Samantha

Samantha

When forces from beyond join us for the greater good.

Cheryl Campbell

Icons Media Publishing

Chapter 1

Sam sat bolt upright. Cold sweat covered her body as her fringe ran wet. She choked as she gasped for air. Her gasping sounds and mumbled words once again disturbed Dave. She had seen this woman before, now here she was again, as clear as day. The woman appeared to be in her 40's, her lips painted red, her face surrounded with auburn hair. Her face wasn't familiar to Sam, which in a way made these appearances ever more frightening. Why was this happening? Night after night these disturbances repeated themselves, showing no signs of stopping.

'Go back to sleep!' Dave mumbled.

Tearfully, she said, 'I don't know what is happening.'

'Then get some help!'

Every morning Sam woke up tired and irritable and as if on autopilot she got herself and Alfie organized. Now they were on the school run. She leaned up looking into her rear-view mirror and glanced at Alfie in the back seat. He smiled back. He enjoyed school and was a bright and happy child she was incredibly grateful for that, as dropped off he was soon surrounded by friends and was ready to run off with them.

Once again, she spent the day in a daze, wondering what

was happening to her, was she imagining things, or worse, going mad!

Refusing to believe either of those thoughts was easy, for she'd always been a bright, organized person, holding down a demanding and stressful job, coping really well. Humming the tune playing through her headphones the same lady's face appeared before her again frightening her two-fold, for now she was sure of being wide awake. This was defiantly no dream.

'Go away!' The woman's face began to fade, but not before Sam saw her lips move, this made her yet more worried, now believing that the lady was trying to tell her something, but what?

Sam smelt burning. Dave's shirt sleeve was scorched. She will have to buy him a new one. The ironing now finished she headed for the kitchen. On her way she noticed that the local newspaper had arrived and picked it up. Flicking through its pages at the dining table, hot coffee in hand her

eyes were drawn to the obituary pages where she glanced down the columns of the deceased. Then it happened, the haunting face of the lady jumped out at her, they were staring into each other's eyes.

Sam read through the details before her. The lady's name was Tanya Tandy. Date of birth, death and a few other details were also noted. She studied the details over and over again, at least now she knew this woman wasn't in her imagination, or indeed she wasn't going mad. Most of all she had something tangible to show Dave. She quickly printed out the page, feeling that if she wasn't quick enough it would disappear, just like the images in her mind. With some sort of relief, she fell asleep quickly that night, enjoying her most peaceful night's sleep in a long time.

The following morning Sam woke feeling refreshed and relaxed, with a sudden 'knowing' within her. Dave was pleased to see her so much happier. That morning even their goodbye kiss had more tenderness than of late.

Once the house was quiet and empty again Sam took out the printed sheet and studied her visitors face and name. Tanya Tandy aged 40, she continued reading, there were a few more details, but most important to Sam was the funeral details for now there was a point of contact.

Trembling hands did not help when trying to tap in numbers on her mobile.

'How may I help?' These where the first words she registered. Sam explained that she needed to get in touch with a relative of Tanya Tandy.

'We can't pass out personal information, sorry, but we can ask our funeral contact, the deceased sister, in this case, to return your call. Would you like to leave your details?'

Leaving her mobile number seemed natural, it was later that she sat and worried. How was she going to introduce herself? How could she possibly tell her of what's been happening to her? How would she cope with what Sam had to say, not that she would believe her in the first place, would she?

She tried to have a normal day but could not concentrate on anything. In boredom and frustration, she finally put the television on, staring at it in a daze. Suddenly, she jolted back into the present, as the programme just starting was about the afterlife. Now her attention was grabbed, for she felt that this was her way forward, a suitable way in which to approach the grieving family. Her 'knowing' was beginning to come to pass. It might have been a coincidence, it didn't seem so though, for as soon as the programme ended her mobile rang.

It was Tanya Tandy's sister Carol. She introduced herself. Their conversation flowed easily it was as if they had known each other all their lives. Sam began explaining to Carol about all that had been happening to her, about seeing her sister and feeling as if she had a message to pass on. To Sam's surprise Carol didn't retreat back in shock and horror, instead she asked. 'Do you mind if I ask you if you believe in Spiritualism?'

'No. I mean I don't really know. I've heard and read about it, but don't really understand what it is all about'. They talked some more, and before she knew it, Sam had agreed to go to a Spiritualist Church that same night with Carol. She did not say too much to Dave, only saying that if it's ok, she'd like to go out with a friend that evening.

'You'll have to keep an eye on Alfie.' He smiled.

'That will be really good for you love, and we'll be fine. You go out and enjoy yourself.'

Relieved that he didn't ask too many questions, enjoying herself was left to be seen, she had no idea what this evening out may bring. Speaking earlier, Carol had suggested that they meet at her house as Sam had to pass it on the way to the church and they could then go together.

Chapter 2

Sam now stood at Carol's front door and knocked. Realizing they were late Carol grabbed her car keys and they were soon on their way. Sam could feel the tension, the dryness in her mouth, that feeling of being more than just nervous, perhaps even feeling scared. As if reading her mind Carol said.

'You'll be fine, nothing to worry about.' Neither spoke further; soon they arrived at the church. Following Carol's lead, Sam collected aa hymn book and sat beside her, the atmosphere being very peaceful and relaxed. People came in, chatted, and nodded hellos!

Promptly at 7.30 the church leader stood up and the proceedings began. Sam swallowed hard and nervously joined in with the first hymn, she continued to follow the service riveted to her seat.

When it was time, the medium of the evening took to the platform introducing herself as Jade. She addressed the congregation by explaining what her role was, which was to bring evidence that there is life after death. This, she explained came to her through clairvoyance, her being able to see things beyond the range of most people, and also by images appearing in her mind's eye, 'but there are various ways in which each individual medium works', she added. Sam flinched. Wow! That was how I saw my lady, she thought.

'And clairaudience, hearing disembodied voices, the ability to hear spirit voices.' Sam flinched again. I saw her lips move. I was halfway there!

'They give me signs and messages from the other side, these I pass on to you continued Jade. Sometimes these messages are easy to understand, or we may all have to work a bit harder at getting them transferred understandably, from Spirit onto me, then onto you.'

Sam was surprised at some of the expressions used by the medium, they were all new to her, but she soon worked out their meanings, and was also astonished at the congregation's reactions upon receiving their messages. There were tears and laughter, yes and no's, even don't know, or may be, as people listened intently to their messages. Sometimes information came in pieces and had to be fitted together, rather like a jigsaw puzzle. Other times perhaps the message did not make sense, but the recipient was usually happy to take the message away with them, and think about it further, or if necessary, discuss it with family members or friends who may be more aware of the issues mentioned. Carol and Sam stopped after the service for tea and biscuits. Many people seemed to know Carol, each spoke to her quietly and gently as Sam stood beside her listening, and hopefully learning. Sam could not tell if they knew of Carol's sister Tanya.

They were about to leave when they saw Jade walking towards them. They stopped and chatted. Jade said that she had a message for both of them and the message was from someone whose name began with a 'T'. Sam's colour drained. Carol gently touched her arm as Jade continued.

'She passed over fairly recently and wants to tell you that you have to go to the police.' It was now Carol's turn to go pale, and even shake a bit, as Sam looked at her in horror saying.

'I don't know anything about this, how have I become involved? Speaking so loud without realizing it meant that the gentleman in charge of the evening rushed over and ushered the three into a small quiet room. He left, returning quickly with a glass of water for each of them, as smiling gently and politely he left the room again.

Carol's eyes were filled with tears, with her voice thick with emotion she said to Jade. 'Please, carry on.'

In shock Sam watched Jade as she listened, and then repeated the words she had just heard.

'Carol, your sister Tanya is here. She wants to tell you that she was poisoned. She says, 'you couldn't have known, please don't feel guilty'. She thinks that there is still some wine in the fridge at her flat. Get the police to check it, please, for she now needs to rest in peace.'

Jade sipped some more water and gently said. 'I'm sorry. I can only give you what comes through.'

'I know said Carol. All my family, Tanya included are medium's, but not many people know this.'

Sam was still in shock, yet she could not contain herself.

'What has all of this to do with me?'

Quietly, Carol said. 'You are also a medium. I've known

it since I first spoke to you. I didn't think you would get so involved, but here we are, sorry.'

'But why didn't Tanya come directly to you with her message?' Carol and Jade looked at each other, as Jade continued. 'Sometimes those close to the deceased are just that, too close, and in the relatives or friends state of bereavement they couldn't deal with a dreadful situation such as this. Tanya, as a medium, would have realized this, and so she looked to you for help.' Carol could see that Sam was filled with utter confusion and suggested she give her a ring and that later they could meet up. They can talk; discuss all that has been taking place. Carol herself was emotionally exhausted. She wanted to go home and have some thinking and release time for herself. Sam realized how upset Carol was, as on the drive home she saw Carol's hidden tears trying to escape.

'I'm so sorry about everything said Carol. I'll ring you soon.'

Dave was dozing on the sofa. He stirred awake, stood up and gave Sam a kiss asking if she had a good night. Sam smiled, saying nothing, as Dave headed upstairs to bed, giving her a chance to relax with a cup of tea and some time to think. Thinking was definitely overrated, for although her mind was ablaze with thoughts, it was just too much to comprehend all at once. Bed seemed a good consolation and to her surprise Sam slept very well, awaking early and refreshed the following morning.

The smell of bacon and eggs wafted upstairs. Dave headed towards Sam in the kitchen and kissed her.

'I'm sure your lips taste better than breakfast he said, but this morning I get to have both!' Alfie appeared downstairs. They sat together, father and son, as Dave ate his cooked breakfast and Alfie his cereal. Sam joined them with Alfie seated in the middle.

Before leaving for work Dave ruffled Alfie's hair, saying. 'My two favourite people together.' He kissed Sam's nose just as he used to, as Alfie looked at them saying 'yuk!' Both parents laughed.

Chapter 3

Sam returned home after the school run to a messy kitchen but it was soon cleaned and tidied, so she headed for the local library. Making herself comfortable in a cosy, soft, seat she glanced at her chosen books, these were on initiation, psychic information, meditating, and much more. Her brain began to get overloaded far too quickly. It was time for her to stop reading, she borrowed some books instead. She hunted through her handbag for her library card feeling silly as she watched someone else using theirs. The lady held her card underneath a light beam which picked up a signal, and then bleeped acceptance. Realizing her library card was the old-fashioned cardboard type, she sheepishly headed for the librarian's desk. Seeing her old card, the librarian said, 'Don't worry, we'll soon sort you out', and quickly handed her a brand-new electronic card. Walking away happily there was almost a spring in Sam's step and a rush of excitement in wanting to learn more about her experiences, for it seemed that the fear of the unknown was holding her back but knowing what she was facing and what possibilities lay before her would make her feel much more able to deal with whatever came her way.

Rushing home, she got stuck into the books, but time

ran away with her, it was soon time to collect Alfie from school. She put her books away from prying eyes and wondered what Dave would think of her reading material. No doubt he would think *I am right; she is going mad!* She didn't get a chance to look at her books all evening, but tonight they were more like the family they used to be. They helped Alfie with his homework, then watched children's television with him, and got him ready for bed. His bedtime story was surrounded by fun and giggles.

Sam woke up thinking about Carol, wondering if she'd been to Tanya's flat yet and if she had been in touch with the police, just at that moment the phone rang. It was Carol asking if she had time to meet for lunch. Carol looked pale and drawn as the two women hugged each other in hellos! Carol speaking first.

'I looked in Tanya's fridge. I did find an open bottle of wine. Seeing it made me feel creepy after what Jade had said. I've never, ever, felt like that before.'

'You should have asked me to go with you, I would have, you know.'

'I know, but I had to do this on my own. You are so lucky Sam you have a lovely husband and son. I have no one.' A tear spilt down Carol's face. Sam pressed her finger against it, wiping it away.

'Sorry! I can see people looking at us.'

'I don't care. Let's go back to mine.'

At Carol's they talked, sharing their thoughts and feelings. 'I haven't contacted the police yet, but I feel I should', said Carol.

'What have you done with the wine bottle?'

'I took it out and looked at it. I wanted to make sure that it was not empty, and then returned it to the fridge. I got too upset to do anything else.' Sam persuaded Carol to phone the police. She did so, explaining nervously that she had information about the murder of her sister. The police personnel at the station took a lot of details about Carol and the so-called victim, his words, after which he said someone would be in touch. Carol and Sam went into the living room. It seemed as if they had just got comfortable when Carol's mobile rang.

'Detective Thomas Campbell speaking; is that Mrs. Carol Glover-Smyth?'

'Yes', said Carol, nervously. Detective Campbell seemed to listen, but Carol detected that he wasn't convinced of her story.

'In any event, we need you to come down to the station to sign an official statement. 10.00 AM tomorrow ok'?' She agreed and Sam was going to accompany her.

Sam collected Carol and drove to the police station arriving just before their appointed time. They were led into a small office. Detective Campbell entered the room with a file tucked under his arm, introducing himself to both women he sat down while opening his file and handing a document to Carol. 'The Death Certificate he said. It states cause of death, heart attack, nae crime there, hen.' Carol winched in surprise and shock. His rough Glaswegian accent did not help her anxious, pent up feelings. 'What makes you think your sister's death was a crime?

'I was given this information.'

'By whom?' Carol shrugged. How do you tell someone that your information came from the dead victim? 'Can't you just check the bottle of wine in the fridge? I was told that's where the answer lays.'

'What for, poison? Asked Detective Campbell.

'Maybe. Carol struggled to speak. She took a deep breath. Poison, yes, that's what I believe.' Sam saw a tear appearing in Carol's eye and gently rubbed her arm in comfort.

'We need witnesses, neighbours to interview, friends, and family of the victim to talk to, the general public to offer information' continued the Detective.

'I don't know anymore. Can't you just check the wine? She began to cry uncontrollably.

'Leave it with me. I'll see what I can do.' Not able to cope anymore, Carol ran out the door with Sam close behind. They sat in the car together, both trying to compose themselves. After a minute or two Sam asked, 'ok?'

'Get me home, please', replied Carol. Sam was about to start the engine when a face appeared at her side window. Startled, she saw the red, rugged face of Detective Campbell. Lowering her window, she said. 'Detective Campbell, you made me jump.'

He tried to smile, but the smile did not appear.

'Please tell your friend I'll dae ma best' he said. Next to her Carol held her face in her hands and sobbed. Sam thanked Detective Campbell as she slid away from the police station carpark.

Chapter 4

Sam left Carol at her front door; they waved to each other as Carol let herself in. They both knew they needed time alone, and either, would phone when the time was right. Their friendship and understanding of each other was growing immensely under all these bizarre circumstances.

A few days later Sam got a phone call from Carol saying that the police had been to Tanya's flat with her, they took away the wine bottle to send to their laboratories for various toxin tests to be conducted. She felt tearful and down, Sam could sense this in her voice, and who could blame her?'

'Will you come to the Spiritualist Church with me this evening?'

'I'm sorry I can't Carol, its Dave's night out with his friends, but if my company will do, you could come here, I put Alfie to bed at 8.00pm.'

'Won't Dave mind? And can I meet Alfie?

'No, Dave won't mind, and of course you can meet Alfie'. They laughed together, for a moment the sadness and tension leaving Carol's voice. By the time they had finished talking Sam had persuaded Carol to have dinner with her family, later Dave would go out, and she could help her put Alfie to bed. Sam hoped that she wasn't pushing their friendship too far too fast but felt that Carol didn't want to be on her own too much. She gave Dave a quick ring at work, he didn't mind company, but just liked to be told what to expect. Sam cooked something homely and simple she wasn't out to impress Carol in any way. A roast chicken with trimmings is what she settled for. Entering Sam's front door Carol could smell the lovely smells of home cooking. She remembered how often, recently; she had been eating pre-cooked meals. Since Tanya's death so much of her had become disinterested in life. They were close, the two sisters, meeting up as often as they could, and talking every day on the telephone. Looking around Sam's home she wondered what they found to talk about but smiled at the thought that they had.

Sam returned with a glass of white wine poured from the bottle which Carol had brought with her. They both felt strange as they clicked glasses, saying nothing, both probably thinking about Tanya. Luckily, the tension was broken as Alfie dashed into the room talking excitedly about his newly built Lego model.

'Look!' He said, shoving it into Carol's hand as she sat on the sofa, almost knocking her wine over. He plonked himself beside her, as Sam took Carol's glass and placed it on a side table.

'I'll just check dinner.' Upon her return they were best friends. Carol tickling him and Alfie giggling like a little girl.

They heard the key in the front door as Alfie scrambled off the sofa and ran into his daddy's arms for a cuddle, Dave then standing him back on his feet, as he ruffled his hair. This seemed like a father son connection.

Sam walked over and kissed Dave, saying, 'this is Carol.'

'Hello! Carol where did you two meet?'

'While shopping', Sam smiled.

Carol was surprised at this answer, but tried not to show it, as they shook hands and shared a few more pleasantries. Dave soon excused himself and went upstairs, taking Alfie with him to wash his hands before dinner.

Hearing Sam serving up, Carol joined her in the kitchen. Sam whispered, 'I had to think of something quickly. I thought that was the easiest explanation.'

Carol nodded sadly, 'Yes, the easiest', they understood each other.

Alfie wandered into the kitchen taking his usual place at the dining table. Dave pulled Carol's chair out for her and pushed it back, as she settled herself in. Time seemed to pass quickly, just chit-chat keeping them going, as Carol remarked what a good cook Sam was.

'The best!' said Alfie, as he tucked into his roast potatoes.

'You have wonderful table manners Alfie, said Carol; you are such a lovely boy.'

'I get told off otherwise.' They all laughed at the innocence of Alfie.

Carol helped Sam clear away, as Sam loaded the dishwasher, while Dave and Alfie sat at the dining table talking. Carol could hear them in the background, but her mind was slowly drifting back to Tanya and also to their childhood.

Her thoughts were interrupted by Sam saying, 'Thanks for that' as she popped a washing tablet into the dishwasher and shut the door. She was switching it on when Alfie ran over and showed Carol his book.

Dave returned downstairs, had a few more words with them, then heading out he kissed Sam goodbye saying he wouldn't be late.

He smiled at Carol. 'You two seem good friends, and she could do with that.' He winked at Sam.

With Alfie asleep almost before his head could touch the pillow, Carol did not get a chance to read him a bedtime story.

They now settled downstairs talking as if they had been friends forever. Sam could not believe how connected they had become, so Carol explained to her the belief of synchronicity in Spiritualism, where somehow things fall into place, where the right people meet each other at the right place and time of their lives. Sam was becoming more and more interested in Spiritualism and showed Carol the books she had borrowed from the library. They discussed various aspects of Spiritualism, some arears Carol could explain, others she said was more about belief. Not everything and every experience could be proved she said and in any case, life is an on-going experience of living and learning.

'I'm sure beginning to see this.' The wine had long gone, they were on coffee and cake, and now Dave's key was in the front door. Sam quickly hid the books behind the cushions as Dave came in. He seemed surprised to see Carol still there.'

'Do you know its midnight?'

'I was just leaving!'

'Oh no! Carol, I didn't mean it like that. I thought that you really didn't realize how late it was.' He blushed.

'No, it is late' said Sam, as she helped Carol into her coat. They walked together as Dave watched, still stunned as to how well they got along. Sam waved to her as she drove away and returned to the living room. Dave hugged her.

'Sorry', said Sam we really didn't realize the time.' Dave smiled in return as they walked up stairs together.

Chapter 5

After the school run the following day Sam phoned Carol. There was no answer. Retrieving her books from their now hidden place, she sighed with relief at Dave not finding them. I must be more careful or think seriously about talking to him about what was now becoming a real interest, paranormal occurrences', spiritual beliefs and all the surrounding issues. Too heavy, she thought, all is going well with us as a family, why bring problems our way? The phone rang making her jump, for all her concentration was focused on one of the books.

'Hello!'

'Sam, you ok? You sound strange.'

'I'm ok, just away in my head. How are you?

'I'm just back from the police station' with this statement Carol burst into tears.'

Stay there, I'll be right over'. Hiding her books, she grabbed her keys and headed to Carol's. Carol watched from her window, she was in too much of a state to answer the door to anyone except Sam. Tears were pouring down her face, her eyes were already red and swollen, and she was shaking. Sam stepped inside and shut the door behind her while taking Carol into her arms. She rocked her gently, allowing here tears to flow, neither saying a word. After a while Carol calmed down, holding hands they went into the kitchen. Sam sat quietly and waited, as Carol, in what seemed in a state of shock, automatically made tea.

Each stared into their own cups for a while until Carol choked as she said. 'It seems she was murdered.' She burst into tears again. Sam put her arms around her.

'I'm here for you, but I just don't seem able to do enough.'

Carol pulled away, so as she could speak. 'You're smashing, thanks for being here for me.'

They did not talk again for a while; the silences seemed to be necessary for both of them. 'What will happen now, what did the police say?' Sam finally asked.

Carol took a long, deep breath. 'It seems that the toxin tests showed that there were vast traces of cyanide in the wine sample, this poisons a person's system, death taking the form of a heart attack, hence, Tanya's death certificate stated, cause of death heart attack. There was no need to have a post-mortem at the time, now the only way to check this would be to see if this toxin was also present in her body.

'Oh! God! Sam gasped. Does that mean you have to take Tanya out of the ground?'

'What am I going to do? 'Sam was shocked herself, she just sat, numbed. Finally, she said.

'Carol, please think of what Tanya would have wanted.

'It must be what she wants. Tanya appeared to you, not me, telling you to get the wine checked!' she yelled. Realising what she had done, she immediately apologized.

'Sorry Sam' I didn't mean to take my frustrations out on

you.' Sam nodded in reply, trying to give Carol some sort of a reassuring smile. They sat quietly for a while. What would you do in my place Sam?'

'I honestly don't know. Carol continued, I do know we can, what they call exhume her body.'

'Dig it up?' asked Sam, with a shiver.

'But I will need special permission' continued Carol, what they call a licence. It means there are a lot of people to contact and a lot of paperwork to do, never mind the heart ache which goes with it all. I need to sit and think, maybe we can talk later?'

I understand', said Sam, as tears poured down Carol's face and she gulped hard trying to stop, or at lease slow them down. Sam drove home in a state of confusion, she was shocked to see Dave's car in their drive. Rushing in she wondered what was wrong.

Dave was seated in the living room he glared at her as she walked in.

'What?'

'I had to leave a very important meeting, that's why you are at home Sam! Alfie's not been well, the school called me as they couldn't get a hold of you.'

'My mobile is on, honest! She stared at it. No signal, battery is dead, sorry!'

Dave glared at her even harder. 'I'm going back to work; you'd better check on our son.' He was gone; Dave was good at that, leaving really quickly. Sam climbed the stairs and checked on Alfie. His face was very red although he was sound asleep. She felt his forehead, he was extremely hot. She sat beside him for a while, watching him sleep, thinking how lucky she was to have him. He didn't wake up. She left, returning with a tepid flannel, placing it on his forehead. That will keep him cool. It's good for him to sleep. She kissed his cheek and left his room.

Sitting on the sofa thinking, Sam suddenly felt herself being shaking awake, not realizing that she'd even fallen asleep.

'Mum!' She heard a husky voice, as she looked into the hot flushed face of her son.

'Alfie!' She hugged him, they lay together for a while, cuddling. This feels so good, thought Sam, I never want it to end, until finally she slipped herself off the sofa making sure that Alfie wasn't too near the edge and headed for the kitchen while keeping an eye on him, she noticed that he was dozing and waking up, finally he wandered over to Sam saying that he was hot.

'How about a shower and some nice clean pyjamas you can choose the ones you want to wear.'

He brightened up, but he was certainly not his usual self. Sam gave him a dose of Copal before taking him upstairs. As Sam showered him, he complained of his throat hurting and she noticed his glands were swollen. She dried him and held out two pairs of pyjamas.

'Which one?' she asked. Alfie pointed; it was obvious that it hurt too much for him to talk. Returning downstairs Sam began getting dinner ready. Alfie had already said that he didn't want to eat but was persuaded to have some egg soldiers. He ate what he could, so Sam was pleased that he'd at least eaten something. By the time Sam and Dave sat down to eat Alfie was asleep again on the sofa.

Sam apologised again for not being there for Alfie. Dave was in a better mood now.

'I'm sorry too, he said. You know I don't know what to do when Alfie is not well, I don't know how to look after him sometimes, anyway, how is he?'

'Not too good. Sore throat, high temperature swollen glands, I'll take him to the doctors tomorrow.'

Dave held out his hand, Sam took it. 'Thank you, I don't thank you enough for looking after us.' She smiled as they went upstairs still holding hands. Sam lay in bed thinking about Carol. She hadn't rung. Sam wondered if that was a good or bad sign.

Waking up to the ringing of the alarm, both were surprised to find Alfie in bed between them.

'Did you hear him', Sam whispered.

'Did you?' They both smiled as to how soundly they must have slept, although they knew, that if Alfie had his usual voice, and called for them, they would have certainly heard him. He opened his eyes and looked at each of them in turn before hugging their necks and falling asleep again.

Chapter 6

After a shower Dave went downstairs and was surprised to see scrambled eggs, toast and coffee awaiting him.

'I could get used to this' he said, winking at Sam. They smiled at each other as Sam sat down.

'I should make an effort', she said.

'You're fine love, you don't have to get up with me, and it's just nice when you do.' She noticed that he was in no rush to leave home this time as they kissed goodbye.

Sam checked on Alfie, he was restless, but still in bed, she left him for a while, plugged her mobile in to recharge and headed for the bathroom. She'd just about finished her shower when the house phone rang. Wrapping a towel around her she answered it in their bedroom.

'Can we meet?' asked Carol.

There was a tiny patter of footsteps on the floor as Alfie appeared beside her.

'Carol, I need to take Alfie to the doctors, can I ring you when I've sorted myself out. Would you be able to come here?'

'What's wrong with him?'

'Please don't worry, children often get sore throats and temperatures, he'll be ok, I'm sure. Can I ring you later?'

'Take your time Sam, I'll be here.' They both said bye and hung up.

Sam was told to come into the surgery and the doctor would see Alfie as soon as he could. They were lucky they didn't have to wait too long.

'What will he do, mum? Alfie asked, his voice was now a near whisper.

'I don't know exactly, love, I think that he will feel your throat to see where exactly it hurts. He might also put the tip of a small machine into your ear, to see how hot you are. Nothing to worry about and of-course and I'll be with you all the time. We can then tell daddy what a big, brave, boy you were.' He smiled.

After the examination, much of which was described well by Sam, Alfie was diagnosed with having an ear infection, Sam was given a prescription for a course of antibiotics and was asked to bring him back in a week.

'I'm taking you somewhere special' said Sam. Alfie's eyes lit up.

'Where?' He soon knew where, as the huge toyshop loomed before them. He was really pleased as Sam helped him out of the car, heading for the entrance, but Sam was soon dragged to the Lego section where he picked up a Lego set he'd wanted for a while. Smiling, Alfie said 'Thanks mum', as they started their return walk back to the car.

Alfie played with the box and studied the pictures on it having been told not to open it until they got home. Glancing at him now and again in her rear-view mirror Sam felt much pride and joy, but most of all very lucky. He really was a good, nice, child, much of his own making, as of hers and Dave's. She only hoped he'd stay that way. By the time they reached home Alfie had dozed off again. Helping him indoors, he was soon settled on the sofa with his new Lego beside him. Opening the antibiotics Sam gently stirred him from his doze and helped him sit up and take a small spoonful of it. He pulled a face making her laugh, which made him giggle as well; luckily, he'd swallowed his medicine by then. Laying him back down she went to the kitchen, just then the phone rang.

'Hello!'

'Hi! Carol, yes he'll be fine, just an ear infection.'

'How are you?'

'OK, she said, but to Sam's ears Carol sounded despondent.

'Can you come over, I'll love to see you,' said Sam.

'When?

'How about I make us all a light lunch? Come over whenever you are ready, Alfie and I won't be going anywhere. Alfie popped his head up grinning.

'Who's coming over?'

'Carol.'

'Good! I can show her my new Lego.'

Carol arrived with flowers and more Lego, she entered and hugged Sam handing her the flowers.

She walked over to Alfie, 'look!' he said, showing her his new Lego as she gave him another set.

'What have you forgotten? Asked Sam.

'Thank you' said Alfie, giving Carol a big hug.

'Next time, young man, said Sam, trying to sound angry 'no thank you, no present.'

Alfie looked at Sam embarrassed, as Carol mouthed, 'That's ok', as they smiled at each other.

'What do you want to eat Alfie?' asked Sam, can you manage a sandwich like Carol and me?' He shrugged his shoulders. 'Ok', let's sit at the table and see what happens. Alfie struggled, but in the end he ate well.

Sam and Carol hadn't had any time alone, so as they cleared away Sam whispered that she'll try to get Alfie to go to his bed for a while.

Calling Alfie over he was given another dose of his antibiotics, as Sam said, 'Why don't you go upstairs, do your teeth and put on your pyjamas, a sick little boy like you needs plenty of rest.

'When can I play with my Lego?

'When you feel better'. Alfie dragged himself upstairs. Carol looked at Sam, and then called out.

'Would you like me to read you a story, Alfie?' He came to the banister and smiled down at her'

'Ok! I'll do my teeth you can wait in my bedroom.' He was soon tucked in with Carol reading him a story, he quickly fell asleep.

As Carol came downstairs, Sam had just finished making tea, they settled together in the comfy living room. Carol sat down with a long, sad, sigh.

'You sound so sad, what can I do to help?'

'Sorry, I keep bothering you and you have a family to worry about.'

'What can I do?' Sam asked again.

Carol took a sip of tea, as she replaced the cup on the little side table, she looked at Sam with tears in her eyes. 'I've given permission for Tanya's body to be exhumed.' Sam went over and hugged her.

'That must have been so hard. What made you finally decide?'

'Well, I truly believe that this was Tanya's decision, not mine, and since I've got to know you, I felt that you will always be there for me. I'm right, aren't I?

'Of course, anything I can do, you only have to ask.'

'Will you help me sort it all out? I have researched the Internet and learnt that I can download a form to fill in which will get Tanya's body exhumed, examined and re-buried. It also helps that I am the only family member left and the next of Kin.'

'Gosh! Said Sam, you have really read up on this.'

'I've had to'. She gave a wry smile and shrugged her shoulders. By now she was in a state again, her eyes were red from crying while speaking and she was shaking. Sam guessed that she must be in shock, pleased that Alfie was still asleep.

'I must go, I've taken up enough of your time, and as I keep saying you have a family to look after. Dave will be home before you know it, and you also need to check on Alfie.'

Sam had wanted to ask Carol this for a long while, so she quickly said, 'Have you really got no family, even a distant relative? Carol shook her head as she leaned into hug her.

'When I feel better, I will tell you more about myself, right now I have enough to deal with.'

'Of course,' said Sam, as Carol opened the door and left.

Sam was surprised to find Alfie standing wide awake at the top of the stairs. He looked much better, and must have felt it, for he asked to play with his Lego.

'Only one at a time, ok? Choose which one.' She could hear him mumbling to himself while deciding which one; he opened the one which Carol had given him. Later, they heard a key in the door, Dave walked in as Alfie shouted, 'Look Dad, I just made my Lego.' Dave looked at it closely. 'You are good at this Alfie, and you've got your voice back.' Alfie smiled. Dave ruffled his hair.

By the following morning Alfie was as bright as a button and couldn't wait to see his friends at school. After dropping him off and returning home Sam wondered if she should give Carol a ring. She decided to think about it while having a cup of tea. She had just sat down when the phone rang.

'Hello!'

'Hi! Carol!' There was quiet on the other end. Sam said hello again.

'Sorry! I was stunned. I wondered how you knew it was me.' Sam laughed.

'Just guessed'.

How's Alfie?

'Back at school, do you want to come over?'

'Ok', but there is not much to say, other than I know they have exhumed Tanya's body and she is now with the Coroner.'

'That's ok, we can just talk' and soon Carol was telling Sam about her past life. She went on to tell Sam that she was married, still is in fact, but her husband John died young from a heart attack. They loved each other very much and had a great marriage, seeing Tanya now and then. Suddenly however, Tanya seemed to be around them all the time. Carol didn't know why, she wondered if she'd had a boyfriend who perhaps had left her, but whatever the reason, she was always there. They knew she must be lonely, but the more time she spent with them, the more distant Carol and John's marriage grew. Tanya seemed to be driving a wedge between them, but John couldn't see this and encouraged her to be around, this in turn caused more problems. Carol said that she and John rowed about this often, each blaming the other for being jealous of Tanya. Soon their marriage drifted apart with each going their separate ways. John moved out giving Carol yet more reason to be suspicious. The one tear which first slipped from Carol's eye was now multiplying, Sam handed her a box of tissues.

'You don't have to carry on telling me', she said.

'I want to tell you everything, please let me get it all off my chest'. Sam smiled a half smile, as she leaned forward and gave her a hug. Carol explained what a successful business-man John was owning many businesses, they had plenty of money, but he just didn't seem to understand Carol's need to spend their precious time alone. In the end time did run out, for John died of a heart attack while still young. Crying even more she said, 'I often wonder if he came home to die. He had been gone for a couple of months. I never heard from him, never knew where he was. I had no way of contacting him. Then he suddenly returned one evening, saying he was sorry, that he missed me, was it ok to move back. He actually asked me that! Of-course it was, it was what I always wanted, and so he brought his cases in. We laughed together and ordered a take-away, and from that night on everything was back to being great.'

In all the time John was gone Tanya never got in touch, see why I wondered about the pair of them? Sam nodded. 'It didn't matter anymore, I wanted my husband, and now I well and truly had him back. Sam wondered how Carol kept going, but she guessed it was simply because she wanted to. Naturally, I was devastated when he died but we were to-gether at the end, and for that I am truly grateful. I was glad to have spent his last moments with him; in fact, he died beside me. We were sitting watching television, holding hands, which we often did. He turned and faced me, took my face into his hands and kissed me. 'I love you Carol, I al-ways have, I always will' he said. I was about to make a joke of things, when I noticed that he was still holding my hand, but his head had now slumped back against the couch. I just knew he was gone.' Carol let out a large sob, it seemed as if her emotions burst out. She mumbled the few last words, 'the paramedics worked on him but he was pronounced dead upon arrival at the hospital. I already knew that', she said, now in control. Sam said they needed a cup of tea, and by the time she came back Carol had fallen asleep on her sofa. Knowing that she must be worn out both emotionally and physically Sam covered her with a throw over and left her while she went upstairs to tidy Alfie's room.

Chapter 7

Carol jolted awake. Looking around she wondered where she was for a moment, but Sam came in with sandwiches and tea. 'More tea?' asked Carol.

'Lunch too; you've been asleep for over two hours.'

'I'm sorry, I should go home.'

'Have lunch first', said Sam, offering her a sandwich. Carol smiled, 'You are too good to me.' 'Sure, help yourself to more.' In the end Sam was really pleased to see that Carol had eaten most of the sandwiches, and now she looked refreshed and relaxed.

'I'd better go', began Carol.

'Only if you want to, or you can leave when it's time for me to get Alfie from school.'

'I feel much better now, can I talk some more, it's doing me good, rather than bottling it all up, is that ok with you?'.

'As much as you like.'

'Tanya attended the funeral, said Carol, but at the time I wasn't yet ready to forgive and forget, if indeed there was anything to forgive and forget, so I thanked her for coming and we left separately.

'It was by sheer coincidence that we bumped into each other a few weeks later. I was shocked as to how pale and thin she looked. I realized that she was my sister, what was done was done, we only had each other left, so I asked her to have a coffee with me. I knew she wasn't keen, so I apologized first. I told her that I missed her, asked if we could put the past behind us, pointing out that we were still sisters.' She finally agreed to join me at my place for Sunday lunch. The barriers came down that afternoon and she told me that she was having money problems. She could not afford the payments on her flat as the rent had been raised, she owed the landlord money already. I offered to give her some; she turned me down flat in a very indigent tone of voice. It was obvious now why she looked so ill; the lack of sleep and worry was probably talking its toll.

'I had to think fast and came up with the idea that I could buy her the flat, it would be an investment, it would be in my name and she would pay rent, that way it seemed that it was less like charity and more like an investment on my part, she agreed. We spoke to the landlord and had everything done legally.

Tanya was a smart woman. She knew her job, worked hard, and was soon paying me a good sum back as she climbed the cooperative ladder. It worked out great, and it got us back as sisters, as friends, back onto the right path. Sam sighed, as Carol said, 'have I worn you out?'

'That's ok, as long as you are fine too.' Carol walked over and gave her a hug.

'You have been my rock. I'd better go now, or you won't have any time to yourself before your family appears again. Thanks for lunch, for everything.' They hugged again and said goodbye soon Carol was on her way, waving and saying they will talk soon. Sam was proud of herself she knew that Carol must have felt so much better, leaving with a smile on her face. Sam praised herself thinking that she must be a good listener.

Sam picked Alfie up from school. He was all laughter and chat about playing with his friends again, and the drive home was indeed a very pleasant one, with the evening going very quickly with the family.

The phone rang, it was late.

'Hello! Said Sam half awake.

'It's me, Carol, I'm so sorry to wake you.'

'Who is it?'

'It's ok, Dave. Go back to sleep, love.'

'Sorry Sam, I didn't mean to wake your family.'

'It's ok, what's wrong?'

Detective Campbell rang, he rang earlier, but I was trying to handle this on my own, but I can't.'

'I'll be right over.' Sam shook Dave awake. It's amazing how quickly men switch off.

'What!' It's ok. I have to see Carol can you listen out for Alfie?' Dave opened one eye and glanced at the clock.

'It's 2.00 am.'

'I know, sorry.' Sam kissed Dave and got out of bed. She dressed quickly, grabbing any clothes, and rushed out.

Carol answered her front door and burst into tears.

'It was murder, she was poisoned she blurted out.'

Sam was devastated.

'I'm so sorry Carol.'

We wanted to find out, but this is just so awful.' Carol continued to cry uncontrollably. Sam sat beside her and held her hand; unable to find any other way in which to help her. Carol did not seem as if she wanted to say anymore, but seemed to want someone near her, so Sam continued to sit beside her, hugging her once in a while, until she finally calmed down and Sam managed to go and make both a cup of tea. When they had nearly finished Carol, not having said a word for ages, said.

'I'm ok now. I'm sorry to have got you out so late, or should we say early? You need to get back to your family.'

'I'll stay. Dave gets up for work at 6.30 am, so I'll make sure I'm home by then. I'll leave when it gets bright. How about we each sleep on a sofa? Carol nodded.

'Sorry!'

'Stop apologizing. I am fine with all of this.'

'Dave?'

'Dave will just have to understand.'

You haven't told him anything yet, have you?

'No, but I'll sort something out; I won't tell him anything more than he needs to know. I'll tell him you had bad news. He'll be too busy thinking about work to ask any questions, then tomorrow we'll talk again and see where we go from there, ok?' Carol agreed and by now she'd got a blanket and pillow for each of them. They said good night and although they both seemed to sleep, they were just as restless as each other.

Chapter 8

Sam got home before Dave had woken up. She checked on Alfie and found him snoring quietly, unlike his dad who was very loud about it. The alarm was ringing as she prepared breakfast. Dave appeared, a new man. Showered and dressed he was so different to the man she'd seen in bed not long before.

She smiled to herself at the thought, Dave said, 'Breakfast for me again?'

'Yeah! You deserve it, and these bright mornings seem to get me up early.' Dave kissed her, sat down, and tucked into his scrambled eggs and steaming coffee.

'Might be late', Dave said, pecking her on the cheek, big meeting, will tell you about it later.'

'Would you ring my mobile? I might go for a coffee with Carol.' As she suspected Dave had completely forgotten about their 2.00 am chat and her leaving the house. Luckily, she knew he would have woken up had Alfie called out.

By the time Sam had dropped Alfie at school and returned she was once again wondering how Carol was doing. One part of her wanted to leave Carol alone the other part was afraid to leave her for too long. Carol was so emotional, fragile and alone. Sam feared for her safety.

She stayed at home, did her housework being pleased to have something practical to do, yet time still dragged, not knowing why, she suddenly felt compelled to read her library books. She reached up to the high shelf at the back of her wardrobe and got them down. She then headed for the comfort of the living room where she settled herself down. The first book was called 'Honing Your Psychic Powers' and to her surprise she found exercises to learn and practice. The first exercise required her to shut her eyes, clear her mind, and see if she could pick up on any words or images. At first her mind was full of thoughts of Carol she didn't think that this was anything psychic it was just that Carol was already on her mind. Suddenly a face appeared before her. It was so clear that it made her jump. Her eyes immediately sprang open. The harder she tried to clear the image away, the clearer it became. Grabbing paper and pencil Sam began writing down the description of the person she saw in her mind's eye. Her hand then seemed to take control, as automatically it drew. While studying her work later she realized that the description and drawing matched each other perfectly. It was one and the same person, in words and a sketch! Who that person was she had no idea; she certainly hadn't seen her before. Shocked, she put everything together and put the book back into its hidden spot.

Sam now began to feel very uncomfortable, feeling unsafe and strange she decided to call Carol. If she couldn't get hold of her, she intended getting out of the house anyway. As if in answer to her quandary Carol phoned.

'Hi! Want a coffee? Want to come around?'

'Yes', said Sam, perhaps too eagerly. Is it ok to come over now?'

'Sure, stay for lunch at least, longer if you like.'

'Great! I'll be there.' Sam was shaking by now; she didn't know why. As she left for Carol's she took her writing and sketch pads with her but left them in the car.

Carol hugged her at the front door. 'You don't look too good, are you ok?'

Sam never thought about how she looked, but now felt much more at ease.

'I'm ok', she managed to mumble, but Carol sensed that she was far from it.

Over a cup of coffee and biscuits Carol told Sam that she'd felt much better today and thanked her for staying with her, Detective Campbell had opened a case file and investigations were beginning. They will start by interviewing Tanya's neighbours to see if anyone or any incidents become of interest to them, they would talk to Sam in due course.

Sam picked up her cup and noticed that her hand was shaking; this seemed to get worse. In the end Carol needed to calm Sam down, instead of the other way around.

'What's wrong? Is Dave upset at you because of me?'

'No, no, stammered Sam. I need to go to my car, will you come with me?' *This makes no sense at all* thought Carol; Sam's car was parked literally at the end of her drive; they could see it from the window. Sam stood up, so Carol followed her to the front door.

Suddenly Sam said, 'It's ok, just wait here, but watch me.

Carol stood on the bottom step watching, not knowing

what to make of Sam's strange behaviour. Sam grabbed her psychic books with her papers in it, locked the car doors electronically, and ran back to Carol. She rushed in the front door, Carol having to rush in after her.

'What is wrong? Please tell me! Is somebody following you?' By now both women were in Carol's living room. Sam fell onto the sofa, stuffing her piece of paper into Carol's hand she looked it and went as white as the paper itself.

'How dare you, are you trying to tease me? Do you know who this is?' As Carol screamed at Sam, she suddenly seemed to lose control and slapped her right cheek. She returned her hand to her side meaning to say a sorry, but it never came out.

'Yes, said Sam quietly, it's Tanya.'

'Yes! Carol was still shouting. Where did you get this drawing of her from? How did you get hold of it? Answer me.'

'Please don't get angry Carol, I know this must be a shock, but it just came into my head and I drew it, look! The opened page book on psychic art was held before Carol. That's how it happened; I can't tell you any more than that. There's no explanation of my connection to Tanya, it just seemed to happen.' Carol went over to Sam and hugged her, 'sorry!' she said, as Sam went on to explain how she had felt so unsettled in her own home, and that is why she has been acting so mysteriously.

Are you free tonight? Said Carol. We could go to the Spiritualist church, there is a really good medium on and you might get another message from Tanya.'

It was now Sam's turn to get annoyed. 'Go to your Spiritualist Church! Spirits appearing to me was how all of this started. I couldn't even decide if I was awake or asleep and now, I don't even know if we are safe as a family in our own home, how do you think that makes me feel? Well, it makes me feel guilty as hell. Guilty and angry for allowing myself to get involved with your, dead sister, I may add, dead, and with you, and with all that has happened since then. I should have left well alone, got Tanya out of my head right-away, but of-course the problem was I couldn't, and I can't now. I don't know what to do.'

'I'll come to your house with you when you leave here,' said Carol. Then we can see if you still feel uncomfortable inside.

Not much I can do about it. I have to live in my own home. I am not like you, a rich widow!' Sam turned on her heal and left the house. She got in her car and drove home.

Entering gingerly, she did not know what to expect, if anything, but after the initial insecurity she realized she felt ok, safe and comfortable, that was of the upmost importance to her, so she thanked God, her Angels, and whoever else looked after her. She had left Carol's on bad terms, now they felt the need to have space and time between them. It had been an emotional day all 'round.

Chapter 9

Sam and Dave had a lovely weekend with Alfie. They took him to a theme park with a small zoo, allowing him on lots of rides suitable for his age and height, finishing the day with burgers, chips and ice-cream before returning home. Alfie was happy, excited and felt very grown up, while giving his parents time to themselves as he kept busy. He woke up much later than usual the following morning, giving them a lie-in, until he dived into bed between them, soon falling asleep again. Dave winked at Sam over Alfie's head.

'This is what a lazy Sunday should be like.' All three lay together, calm and contended. Sam finally got out of bed, made breakfast for all of them, and took it upstairs alongside a glass of milk for Alfie.

'Careful!' Said Sam, as she tried to balance the tray as Alfie's flying feet nearly knocked it over. He was playing rough and tumble with his Dad but they soon settled down and had their food.

Alfie was the first to get out of bed and head for the bathroom, so Sam asked Dave if he would help him to shower.

'No mess' she shouted, teasing.

'I don't make a mess mum, its dad,' shouted Alfie. Smiling

Dave went over, ruffled his hair, stripped him down, and stood him under the water.

Sam was surprised to see both of them standing behind her as she turned around from her washing up.

'That's what I like to see, my boys clean and smart', they both smiled.

'We're on a mission' said Dave, got your shoes Alfie?

'What mission?

'Can't tell you mum, it's secret.'

'Oh! ok, then.' They walked out the back door, as Sam headed upstairs.

Ready for the day ahead, Sam returned downstairs to find every cupboard door in the kitchen open, but there was no one to be seen. After her touches with the unknown she was beginning to panic, but then saw Alfie by the dining table. He was trying to suppress a giggle as he went over to Sam, taking her hand, he led her to the table upon which it sat a huge bouquet of flowers in a vase. Sam realized why the entire kitchen cupboard doors where probably left open, they were looking for the vase. Dave crawled out from under the table as Alfie broke into uncontrolled laughter as he stood up rubbing his back and said to Sam, 'I love you.'

Alfie then began jumping up and down excitedly, unable to contain himself, as Dave gave Sam a card and present. Before she could acknowledge it, Alfie handed her a card and gift as well. Sam laughed as Dave stood there, still rubbing his back. Smiling, she bowed to them.

'Thank you, thank you', she said. I don't know which one to open first.'

Alfie helped by holding out his card and saying, 'This one.' Inside was written I love you Mummy. Sam lifted him from his chair next to her and sat him on her lap, then kissed him. Together they opened her present. She felt the tears coming, as inside was a beautiful gold heart shaped ring with a tiny sparkling diamond set in the middle. She looked at Dave. Thank you she mouthed, as Alfie took her hand and gently placed the ring on her finger.

'That was very nicely done, love,' she said.

'Daddy let me practice on Woody in the car', he looked at Dave and scrambled off Sam's lap.

Sam took Dave's hand and squeezed it, then opened the other box expecting to find another ring, instead, it contained a matching set of gold earrings, heart shaped with a tiny sparkling diamond set in the middle, the most beautiful and romantic gifts she had ever seen! 'Thank you', she gave Dave a kiss on the lips, to which Alfie said, 'yak!'

Pulling away gently from Dave, she said, 'I never expected all of this', it was her turn to giggle' and it's not even my birthday!' Dave pulled her onto his lap.

Alfie not knowing what to do said, 'yak!' again while scrambling onto Sam's lap, not wanting to be left out.

Dave laughed saying, 'My thighs are hurting', as Sam gently lifted Alfie off and stood up herself. Dave began pulling strange faces, showing that his legs really did ache, as wife and son led him to the sofa for a soft, quiet, sit down.

Sam went upstairs, Alfie following her. He watched as she gently and lovingly put the earrings in her ears, and holding hands they went downstairs to show Dave, he was lying on the sofa fast asleep.

'Shush!' said Sam, putting her index finger to her lips, 'let Daddy sleep.'

Alfie laughed, 'We wore him out mum', he said.

Alfie got out his Lego and joined Sam at the table where she sat reading the newspaper. Sniffing the flowers, she said, 'these are just beautiful, and I do love you and Daddy. Can you smell the lovely fragrance?'

'Sweet.'

'Yes, it does smell sweet, well done.' Alfie smiled and got back to his Lego as she continued reading the newspaper.

After what seemed like ages, she heard Dave stirring and went to put the kettle on. Once she'd seen him sit up, she took over a cup of tea for both of them and placed it on the side table. Alfie had a glass of juice. 'Thank you', he said, placing his plastic cup alongside theirs. Sam and Dave were seated side by side on the sofa. Alfie wasn't happy with this, so he wiggled his bottom and squeezed himself between them making all of them laugh. All Sam could say was, 'I'm so very happy'; as she stretched her hand behind Alfie in order to touch Dave. She was a very happy, contended person, especially over that special weekend, although feeling as if something would spoil it, and sure enough, just then the phone rang.

'Don't answer it', too late, Alfie was already there, and she hadn't even realized that he could reach it.

'Hello! Yes, we are having lots of fun today, and Daddy has bought Mummy a gold ring and earrings.'

'Enough!' shouted Sam, taking the phone out of Alfie's hand.

'Hello!' Sorry', said Carol, did I get Alfie into trouble?'

'No, not as it is you', she didn't sound very convincing, not even to herself. It's just that Alfie must learn what he can and can't say to people.'

Carol continued, 'I just wanted to say I'm sorry, we left on bad terms, and I don't like that'

'It's ok Carol, I was in the wrong too, let's forget about it. Can I ring you tomorrow, after I've dropped Alfie at school?'

'Please do', said Carol, as they both said a quick goodbye and hung up.

'What's wrong? Asked Dave, you two ok?'

'Just us women, we'll be fine again'. Dave shrugged his shoulders as Alfie asked.

'Can we go to the park? Can I take my bike?'

'Firstly, you and I need to have a grown-up talk,' said Sam. You are never, ever, to talk on the phone like that again, it doesn't matter who you are talking to. Now a bugler knows there is gold jewellery here'.

'But Carol isn't a burglar.'

'Don't you answer me back Alfie!' Instead of going to the park you are lucky that you are not being put into your pyjamas. Alfie looked at the point of tears, as he looked down at the floor.

'Take it easy, love', said Dave. He'll have nightmares about buglers now; he's only 5 years old.'

'I know, I'm sorry, I just worry about my little family.'

'Yes,' said Dave taking Sam's hand, I'll explain things to him gently.

'Thanks' said Sam, as Dave ruffled Alfie's hair to show that all was well. Alfie looked up at Dave, managing a half smile.

Dave and Alfie came over to Sam a while later.

'Sorry mum', said Alfie. '

'I'm sorry too, said Sam, just be careful what you say, ok? Or best of all leave us to answer the

phone.' Dave gave Sam a strange look, as Alfie nodded his head in reply.

'Look! How about we finish off this lovely day with burgers, chips and ice cream. They smiled as Alfie went to put his trainers on.

With Alfie now fast asleep Dave said 'What is it with you and Carol? What was all that big issue about burglars?

'I told you, women fall in and out of friendships. I'll sort it. I'll give Carol a ring tomorrow.'

They sat in silence. Dave not one bit convinced with Sam's answer. He felt in his bones that there was more to this and glanced over at Sam. He could tell that her mind was racing too, both were in deep thought.

'What is it Sam? What's going on? Dave pulled Sam gently into his shoulder to comfort her. She could hear the beat of his heart, steady and firm, like the man himself. There were times she so wanted to tell him everything, but although they were so close, feared his rejection. After all, didn't he say that he thought of her as being strange when she first started telling him about her spiritual connections?

What on earth, would he think of her connection to Tanya? A dead woman whose sister she hangs around with! She shivered thinking about it.

Chapter 10

Dave felt Sam shiver. He kissed the top of her head and lifted her face up kissing her lips long and passionately. It was unexpected, it was lovely, and it was fun and as they both came up for air, they laughed at each other, feeling like teenagers again.

'Tell me everything he said, nothing can make me love you more than I do right now.'

'Fix us both a drink and be prepared for a shock or two.' Sam had suddenly decided that she didn't want any secrets between them but wondered how Dave would react to it all. He seemed lost for words as Sam spoke, telling him how she really met Carol and how her ghost of her sister appeared to her. Speaking quickly, without a breath, exhaustion soon came. Dave listened, saying nothing, leaving occasionally to top up their glasses and when she finally stopped talking, all he managed to say was, 'I hear you, but I don't know what to believe.' Sam shrugged her shoulders in reply as Dave left her there and went upstairs. She presumed that he was going to check on Alfie. She waited and waited but Dave did not appear downstairs again. She found him already in bed and fast asleep, his arm spread across her side of the bed. She took that to be a bad omen, got herself ready for bed and slept in the spare bedroom.

Sam woke up to the noise of the shower and went downstairs, knowing that Dave was getting ready for work she began cooking him breakfast. He came down and kissed her cheek, ate his breakfast, drank his coffee and left. Not a word was said between them, leaving Sam with a feeling of being in limbo and unsettled for the rest of the day, and who could blame her. She longed to ring both Dave and Carol, but with such unsettled emotions she decided against it, while thinking this, the phone rang.

'Hi!' it was Carol.

'What's wrong Sam?'

'I told Dave everything last night, now I simply don't know what he thinks.' There was an unusual silence between them, leading Sam to say, 'I'll ring you back soon, I promise.'

Carol simply said, 'ok', and hung up the phone.

Sam got back into her library books, being unsure of her own beliefs made her wonder why she expected anything more from Dave. Walking cleared her head, as she was about to step out of the door, she heard the phone ringing.

'Hi!' It was Dave.

'Hi! Are you ok?' Yes, but I'm sorry, Sam. I left in a terrible way this morning. Can we go out to dinner, just the two of us, we could just talk quietly.'

'That will be good! Can I ask Carol to come over and sit with Alfie? Or have you gone off both of us?'

'Of course not, that's fine.

Sam phoned Carol back, she apologized and explained.

Carol was over the moon to be asked to look after Alfie it meant that they could all still be friends.

Carol arrived to look after Alfie, and was greeted with the usual hug from Sam. Upon seeing her, Alfie jumped into her arms nearly knocking her over. Laughing, she steadied herself.

'You look stunning!' she said to Sam, noticing her new matching sparkling ring and earrings, the cause of which almost split up their friendship, for Dave resented Sam answering the phone call which interrupted their beautiful family time together.

Dave shook hands with Carol saying hello! and thanking her for agreeing to stay with Alfie. They were both seated and settled watching a movie when Sam and Dave left for dinner.

Talking openly over dinner Dave told Sam that he simply couldn't believe that the living and dead could communicate.

'I feel that I will never understand this concept, but as long as you are alright, and anything you do or say doesn't affect Alfie, I guess you have to do what's best for you at any given time.' Sam understood what Dave was saying and thanked him for being so understanding.

'I don't know what to believe myself, all I know is that what I see and hear is very real, it is defiantly not my imagination. I just know!' she stressed, as the waiter appeared. Each sat with their own thoughts for a while, sipping their drinks, and soon their meal was placed before them. Dave took Sam's hand across the table.

'That was our communication', smiled Sam. You still only

have to touch me, and I melt.' Dave smiled back. They had both said their piece, and so they soon felt at ease again, talking and laughing as the time went quickly by.

Arriving home, Dave went straight upstairs to check on Alfie.

Sam asked Carol 'all ok?'

'We had lots of fun, how about you?'

'Us too' said Sam grinning.

Back downstairs Dave saw Carol getting ready to leave.

'Thanks for staying with Alfie.'

'You're welcome. He really is a lovely boy'.

'We have his mum to thank for that', Dave said taking Sam's hand. They walked to the front door; the two women hugged goodbye before Carol drove away.

Sam couldn't believe the chaos which greeted her first thing the following morning. Dave woke up late and was rushing around in a terrible mood. Alfie seemed, not much better, he didn't want to move himself either, leaving Sam fed up by the time she'd dropped him at school and returned home. It was still only around 9.30 am. And she decided to relax, taking a break before starting on her housework, but she didn't get a chance, the phone soon rang.

Carol was in a state again. Sam said she'll be over and headed off to her house. She was shocked to find Detective Campbell there, talking to her. Tearfully Carol listened as Sam joined them.

'We are going to investigate further into Tanya's death. We have found many, varied, fingerprints on the wine bottle in Tanya's fridge, and in the flat itself. We are now checking these prints against criminal records to see if any match. Neighbours have confirmed the coming and goings of strangers. 'Are you sure you have never met any of your sisters' friends or even any acquiesces?' Asked Detective Campbell.

'No!' said Carol. I feel terrible. I really don't know anymore.'

'Not to worry hen, it's not your fault, he gently pated her arm. I'll be in touch', he said. Carol sighed and realized that this investigation was now taking a completely different turn. Sam walked the Detective to Carol's front door. She felt for Carol. In her head she scolded herself for the moans she had about the terrible start to her day. Nothing of that even came close to what Carol was going through.

'I am so sorry, she said to Carol. You know that I'll always be around for you.'

Carol went to put the kettle on while sniffing, holding back the tears. Drinking tea together was a quiet time, and Carol managed to calm down during the process. Suddenly, Sam felt her arm being grabbed.

'There's still time, come on! They were on their way out of the door and already in the car before Sam realized what was happening. It was only then did Carol say sorry! We're going to the Spiritualist Church, is that ok? I hope you don't have anything else to do.' She continued driving.

Upon them entering the Church Carol was greeted by many people. Sam wondered once again why none of them had a closer friendship with her. The service started; soon the medium was on platform. Sam was proud of herself for remembering the sequence of the service, and even the hymns. Amongst other messages, the medium looked at both of them and said. 'There is a light between you. This person wants to talk to both of you.' They looked at each other as the medium continued. 'This lady wears bright red lipstick, she is not telling me anymore about herself. She simply says. 'All will be revealed, be patient.' They smiled at each other and thanked the medium in unison.

At the end of the service, they both came out revitalized and full of hope that justice will be done for Tanya.

Laughing now, Carol apologized again.

'I didn't mean to almost kidnap you, but it was worth it. Wasn't it'?

'Of-course. What made you suddenly rush off to the service?'

'Tanya! I heard her voice in my head telling me to go. So, we went!'

Sam did not go back into Carol's house; they had their customary hugs as Sam got into her car and drove home. Entering her kitchen, forgetting that the breakfast dishes had not been cleared away, she got on with doing them and had just finished loading the dishwater as the phone rang.

Chapter 11

'Hello!' 'Mrs. James?'

'Yes. I'm afraid Alfie isn't too well, perhaps you can come and collect him.'

'Right away' said Sam and left. She felt relieved that she was at home and not at Carol's or at have church with her mobile switched off.

Alfie looked red-faced and sweating, just sitting and waiting. She bent down and cuddled him as the receptionist watched before waving them off. Sam asked Alfie what was wrong. He didn't answer. Assuming that his throat may be hurting, she drove home, smiling at him through her rear-view mirror occasionally. She received a wide-eyed look in return. Getting indoors Alfie headed upstairs. Sam took him to the bathroom, helped him do his teeth and got him ready for bed. He took himself to his bedroom while Sam grabbed the Calpol from the bathroom cabinet. She was shocked to find him asleep upon her return but managed to sit him up and get some down him, and gently lay his head on his pillow, giving him a cuddle and kiss on his cheek. He smiled at her with heavy eyes and fell asleep instantly. Sam worried about how tired he seemed to be. How desperately he seemed to be in need of his bed and felt her need to be close by. If his throat was that sore, he wouldn't be heard if he did call out. To give herself peace of mind she made herself comfortable in their bedroom instead of going back downstairs. Keeping busy she once again got into reading the psychic books, still fascinated by how much of what she was reading was happening more often in her own life.

Later, Sam checked Alfie again. He was still asleep, and extremely hot, so hot to the touch that it frightened her. She could feel her hand burn sharply at the mere touch of his forehead she immediately placed a cool flannel on it and sat beside him. Suddenly, he began groaning, muttering, and shaking violently. She realized he was having a fit of some sort. Panicking she wondered what to do next. Should she call the emergency services? Or dive him to a hospital? Sam's mind was in a whirl, her face covered in tears, as leaning over him she cried. 'Alfie, darling, what is happening to you? What's wrong?'

She heard the key in the lock downstairs and shouted. 'Dave come up quickly.' Hearing her call, he dashed up the stairs two at a time. Taking one look at Alfie he said, 'I'll carry him out, you get the car started!' She ran downstairs, got the car started, and in soaking pyjamas Alfie was rushed to hospital.

He was soon on a bed in A&E. They paced the floor waiting for a doctor to arrive. It seemed like ages, but it was probably only a matter of minutes before he was seen. Alfie was admitted immediately. Sam and Dave stood nearby, as the doctors examined him. They talked amongst themselves, making his parents angry.

'He's our son', shouted Dave, tell us what is happening!'

A nurse came over and stood beside them. 'Please she said, it's going to be a while yet and we need to take some blood for testing.'

'But what's wrong?' asked Sam in a nervous, tearful voice.

'We'll find out, the doctor will talk to you as soon as he can.' When the staff had moved away, they went to Alfie. He lay very still, looking very pale. His look frightened them. The doctor began to explain.

'We believe he is suffering with recurring infections of the nose and throat. We are going to insert a drip and pump antibiotics into him they will get into his system quicker and be more effective.

In the meantime, the blood tests should tell us more about what is happening inside him. His breathing is shallow but the antibiotics will help correct that.' Sam tried holding back the tears, but they fell anyway. Dave placed a protective, loving, arm around her, holding his own tears at bay.

'You are welcome' to stay' the Doctor said. The staff will help you sort things out.'

They sat beside Alfie, each holding a hand. He knew nothing of what was happening. Sam finally convinced Dave to go home and relax. Get something to eat. He had been working all day and must be hungry. He agreed to leave on condition that he would get changed, freshen up, and bring food back so as they could eat together.

Dave and Sam nibbled at their food, more worried about Alfie than being hungry. Nurses came in and out checking on Alfie throughout the night. All they said, when asked, was that he was doing ok. Early the follow morning Sam was relieved that Alfie's temperature had dropped. He was normal to the touch. She saw this as a good sign. She spent most of the day by Alfie's bedside and it was only after Dave had visited in the evening that they both went home together.

Returning home, they seemed to need to hold each other. That human warmth and comfort seemed so important. Eventually Sam said. 'I don't know how this happened so quickly, he just seemed to have a convulsion for no apparent reason'.

'Remember love, said Dave, they did say a high temperature can bring on a fit, and that is probably what happened.'

Sam nodded, 'I forgot.'

Sleeping restlessly Sam suddenly jumped fully awake, sensing that the phone was about to ring. It was as Sam suspected. The hospital was asking them to go in. By the end of the call Dave was dressed and on his way downstairs, she followed quickly, not caring about what she looked like.

The doctor was on the ward with Alfie. He took them a side and said. 'I'm afraid Alfie is having trouble breathing, we think it would be best to place him on a ventilator. Sam grabbed Dave's hand. He felt her trembling.

'Come with me', said the doctor, leading them into a more comfortable room. They sat close together, as the doctor continued. My staff are sorting things out now, and he will be moved into intensive care where he can be watched closer.

'But what is wrong?' they asked.

'A very bad chest infection. The ventilator will give him a rest and will do his breathing for him, just for a while.' His body will rest and recover. Looking at Sam he said, it is only for a while. I know it all looks very scary Mrs. James, but it is for the best.'

'Is there any other medication involved? Asked Dave

'Yes, he's still on antibiotics and we may need to change or increase the dosages. I know this is very worrying. You can stay at the hospital or come and go just as you please. Alfie will be assigned a nurse who will help you with every-thing and keep you informed. I'm sorry, but I must go now.' Shaking his hand, Dave thanked the Doctor. They sat down again, not saying anything, just holding hands, until a nurse appeared. She said she would take them to see Alfie. What a shock they got! Alfie looked so small and fragile amongst the machines. The loud noises added to their fear. Guilt and yet more worry added to Sam's guilty conscious.

They looked at Alfie unbelievably, as the nurse explained the equipment, most of which went over their heads. They stood beside him, holding his hands one minute, stroking his face the next. Dave even ruffled his hair. He just lay there, ever so still. The nurse reassured them that he was simply resting. She showed them the kitchen, another comfortable room, and the general area, which prompted Sam to ask. 'How long will Alfie be in here?'

'We'll have to see how he does' said the nurse, she smiled, you can make yourself comfortable. You don't need to be near his bed all the time. You will meet some of the other parents too.' Sam threw her a nasty look. What she felt like saying was I'm not here to meet other people! My son is ill. All I want is him healthy and home.'

It was an awful time for Sam and Dave. They were told on another day that Alfie will be put under sedation and that too, will help his body rest and recover. Once again Sam was in a panic and by now at the hospital every day. Dave joined her in the evenings they went home together every night, sleeping lightly just in case the phone should ring. They were told that Alfie could hear them perfectly although he couldn't respond, but it was important that he knew that they were there. Sam talked, read and even sang to him quietly, slowly beginning to feel more comfortable in the hospital environment. She talked to him about his Lego and promised to buy him more upon his return home.

In the meantime, Carol was going frantic. She could not get hold of Sam. She rang, went to her home; she tried this at various times, over many days and even dropped a note through her letter box. Still no response.

Dave found mail under his feet as he walked in the front door. Looking down he was shocked to see the amount of mail lying around, and to realize that he hadn't noticed this for days, his mind probably being totally absorbed with thoughts of Alfie. At work he was distracted. His boss and some colleagues knew about Alfie so they understood and covered for him where and when necessary.

Dave finally started sorting out the mail while the kettle boiled. He'd had a shower, changed, and thought he'd make himself a decent cup of tea before returning to the hospital. He found the note addressed to Sam and wondered if he should take it into her. He decided against it, figuring that if Sam wanted people to get hold of her, she would leave her mobile on, but he had noticed it was switched off all the while now. He was sitting at the dining table with his tea when the phone rang. Like Sam he didn't want to get involved with too many other people so decided to let the answering machine pick it up, he could ring the caller back if necessary.

Dave was greeted with good news as he arrived at Alfie's bed side. He could see that he'd been taken off the ventilator and Sam told him that they were slowly bringing Alfie out of his sedation. Suddenly Alfie said, 'Mummy, Daddy', as he saw them beside him.

They both looked at him in shock at first, but quickly hugged and cuddled him, Sam saying 'Hello darling! It's lovely to hear your voice again.' Dave ruffled his hair. They were over the moon to see him lively again, as the nurse went to let the doctor know that he had come round.

The doctor examined Alfie as they stood close by. Alfie was all smiles, very interested in what the doctor was doing, asking him questions. They knew that he was truly on the mend now. The doctor was really pleased with his progress. He suggested that they keep him in for one last night. Alfie didn't remember much of what had happened but did tell them that while he was sleeping a lady with bright red lipstick kept coming to visit him, she said that he would be ok, he needed to rest. Sam was shocked, but immediately knew who the lady was, as Dave tried to convince Alfie that it was only a dream.

'No Daddy! He insisted, she said that I was a very brave little boy and also said something about Carol. Screwing up his face he said, but I can't remember, I can't remember what she said.' He was beginning to cry.

'It's ok love, don't you worry, it's all ok', said Sam hugging him tightly, as she did, she saw the anger in Dave's eyes. There was silence now, both not knowing what to say, luckily a nurse appeared with Alfie's tea. They smiled at him happily as he woofed down his food and also gobbled down two extra yogurts offered to him by the nurse. With a big smile on his face, he cuddled both of them, happy to feel well again and soon forgot about the lady and her message for Carol.

Dave on the other hand was as mad as hell, and the moment they stepped indoors he spent no time in letting Sam know. In fact, he forbid her to continue her friendship with Carol.

'Let me point out to you, he shouted. I said that nothing you and Carol say or do is to interfere with Alfie in any way. Well? Obviously, it has, so the friendship has to stop. It's to cease right now! If you love me and Alfie that is what you will do.'

'That is blackmail!' shouted Sam.

'A deal is a deal, Sam!' She heard the loud thumps of Dave's footsteps heading upstairs, sounding more like a five-year-old, than a thirty-five-year-old! A hot cup of tea later she was still trying to decide what to do about Carol and was not prepared to put up with Dave's demands, but knew that she had made him a promise. She wracked her brain trying to find a way around the situation. A go-between of some sort, but in the end, she was too tired to think any further, she gave up and went to bed.

Chapter 12

Cooking breakfast the next morning Dave arrived in the kitchen.

'Morning!' she tried to sound cheerful.

'Morn...' mumbled Dave. No breakfast, busy day'. He gulped down his coffee.

'Alfie's home today she said happily.'

'Great! said Dave. I'll see him tonight.' No conversation, or kiss, he was gone.

Sam was in a state, her mind whizzing around. She could not give up on her family but nor could she give up her friendship and her strong involvement in Carol's life. She reflected upon Carol saying that Tanya had chosen her as her messenger believing that she would stay with Carol through thick and thin. Neither could be let down, she would have to sort out these differences to every ones liking.

Watching the clock its hands moving at a snail's pace, at last it was time to collect Alfie from the hospital.

Alfie had not forgotten, 'Mummy, my Lego.'

'How would you like a burger and chips too? Alfie giggled in response.

'Two Treats?'

'Yes, but remember. You have to be an especially good boy.'

'Ok'. Alfie loved his new Lego and his food. She wanted to feed him up. Make him strong again. Burger and chips wasn't the healthiest of meals, but it was a treat after all!'

Alfie raced to Dave as he entered the front door, they

hugged and cuddled. Dave ruffled his hair. Picking him up playfully he put him on the couch.

'Mind my Lego', he shouted.

'Not more Lego!' teased Dave.

'I need to finish building it', said Alfie.

Dave smelt the home cooking.

'Nice smells' he said. Sam kissed him. She tasted his succulent lips.

'Hope my stew is as tasty as your lips' she said shyly. Dave was hooked. 'Quick wash', he said, and off he went. The steaming food was before him upon his return, as Alfie played with his now completely built Lego.

'Look Daddy.'

'Lovely job. You are getting better at this', said Dave. Aren't you eating?

'Two treats', grinned Alfie and he was gone.

'Right! I'm beginning to get the picture. Lovely meal, wine, kisses, forget about the argument and hassle, right?

'Please Dave. Carol is the only friend I have.'

'You could have made friends with any of the other mums, but you never bothered, did you?

'What's wrong daddy? You sound angry.

Dave went to Alfie. 'Bedtime soon', he said, going upstairs abruptly.

When Sam had cleared away, she took Alfie upstairs for bed. Following her Dave said.

'I'll sort it.' He helped Alfie into the shower.

Sam returned downstairs. In time Dave joined her.

'I'll say goodnight to Alfie,' said Sam.

'Come back down, won't you?' asked Dave. Sam thought that his voice seemed softer. She hoped so, at any rate. They sat and talked for a good while, he was still very upset, but didn't want this heavy atmosphere to continue, mostly for Alfie's benefit. Sam told him that she didn't want to break her promise, but she couldn't explain just why Carol's friendship was so important, or why she had got so wrapped up in her life, it simply just happened. It was almost as if it was meant to be.'

'I don't want to know about Carol or her life. I don't want to know about her dead sister. I just want Alfie left out of this Dave said firmly. I want him to be the lovely, innocent child that he is, thanks to you. I don't want him in the middle of anything.'

'I know, I understand,' said Sam. He hasn't mentioned seeing a lady again and if he does, we'll continue with telling him that it was just a dream, ok?'

'Ok. I like Carol too, and Alfie loves her, let's just leave it at that,' said Dave. Sam jumped up giving Dave a playful salute, alongside a wink.

'Bed'! She demanded in fun and he followed her. They had a loving, caring night. Later she woke up remembering that they had not taken any precautions. They laughed and talked upon awaking, as Sam whispered in Dave's ear that there is a chance that they may be a patter of tiny feet in the future. With a wide smile Dave said.

'What will be, will be.'

Sam dropped Alfie at school and with the sun shining she decided to leave the car at home and go for a walk in the nearby park. The walk was good for her, it made her feel rejuvenated. After thinking about things for a while she realized that her and Carol had not been in touch for a few days. It also occurred to her she hadn't seen Tanya for a while. She wondered if being away from Carol meant that Tanya stayed away too, or indeed that neither one of them needed her anymore. These thoughts made her feel sad, confused, and even angry. Was she being used? Why hadn't Carol been in touch? Her head was in a whirl again. Entering her front door, she heard the phone ringing. She rushed to it. 'Hello! Sam. How are you?'

'Not heard from you in a while,' said Sam.

'I've been busy, fancy a coffee?' Sam found herself getting annoyed. Her marriage almost fell apart as she fought Dave in order to keep hold of her friendship with Carol, and all Carol could say was that she was busy.

'I'll ring you back on Friday, ok?'

'Sam, what's wrong?' you sound strange.

Sam hung up. She was really frustrated with the whole business and went upstairs to busy herself. Hearing the doorbell, she looked out of Alfie's bedroom window. She could not see Carol, but she saw her car, and tried to keep calm. When she answered the door, Carol leaned in for their customary hug. Sam pulled away but did gesture for her to come in. Carol saw the look of annoyance on Sam's face. It was now time for Carol to feel hurt and confused.

'What's wrong Sam, please tell me.' Sam was ready to explode.

She fumed. 'I nearly lost my marriage because of you and you haven't been in touch for days.'

'I couldn't 'said Carol quietly. I was in a police cell!'

'What!'

'Yes, I was taken into custody, held there for a whole twenty-four hours. I then figured I ought to get a lawyer, so I've been really busy. They found my fingerprints on the wine bottle, so I am now the number one suspect in my own sister's murder. The police always take the most interest in those nearest to the victim that being me of course. Sam went over to Carol. They hugged each other, as tears fell from both of them. Their tears seemed to wash away their tensions. Carol continued, calmer now. Later, they told me that they had also found quite a few other prints, but all were too smudged and damaged, not suitable for police use in any way. It seems that from public statements that Tanya had a man living with her on and off. When he was there loads of people appeared and it became party time with lots of drink, foul language and much more. So why and when did she spend so much time with us? Was it when he was away? Or when he was at her flat with all these other people? Did she need to get away from him for some reason? If only she had talked to us. John and I could have helped her, even moved her away if necessary, anything she wanted. We failed her, choked Carol. We really let her down. Worst still, I even thought wrong of her and John. What sort of a sister, wife, was I?'

Carol seemed to suddenly become restless. She paced Sam's kitchen floor. Cup of tea in hand. 'Fancy a walk?

There's a nice park close by.' Carol said nothing but followed Sam in putting on her jacket and following her out the door.

It was a sunny, but fresh afternoon. Carol walked briskly. Sam had a job keeping up with her, but the pace and timing seemed to suit Carol's mood. Reaching a bench Sam sat down saying, 'I'm puffed out', not telling Carol that she had already had a walk earlier that day.

'I'll be back', said Carol and carried on in her brisk fashion. Upon her return she still looked sad, but the tears had gone, she looked some-what stronger. Sam was glad to see this, as together they walked, at normal pace, back to her house. They said goodbye at Carol's car and waved as she pulled away. Sam just about had time for a quick tidy around before doing the school run again.

Heading towards the other waiting mums Sam was shocked to see Alfie looking hot and flushed waiting at his classroom door, hand in hand with his teacher.

'We would have phoned you Mrs. James', she said, but it was so near the end of the school day that we thought that we would just keep him quiet and rested until you arrived.'

Sam thanked the teacher, as taking Alfie's hand she said. 'What's wrong Alfie?'

'Don't know mummy'. His husky voice told her that it was a bad throat again. She picked him up and carried him to the car cuddling him along the way.

Upon his return from work Dave wasn't happy at all. He felt that Alfie was ill too often. Sam agreed with him and said she'd take him to the doctor the following day and push for something further to be done for him. It was a quiet evening. Alfie played with his food, while Sam and Dave ate theirs in silence. Sam did eventually persuade Alfie to eat a couple of yogurts, struggling, he managed.

Alfie woke during the night, his temperature was raised, his throat was sore, and now he was crying, rubbing his ear as he wandered into his parents' bedroom for comfort. Dave picked him up, kissing his cheek. 'You sleep here', he said, as Sam tucked him in. 'I'll sleep in your room.'

The next morning Sam woke up to Dave's ringing alarm clock, and turned it off quickly as not to disturb Alfie, half asleep she went into Alfie's room to wake Dave.

Turning over he said, 'I'll be there.' She waited to hear him use the bathroom but heard nothing so went to the bathroom and got herself ready. Only then did she hear Dave moving around, they passed on the landing but said nothing. When she returned to their bedroom Alfie was waking up. 'Go back to sleep, love, you can't go to school today.' He half smiled, closed his eyes and was off in slumber land again. The Calpol must still be working, she thought, while getting herself dressed.

Going down to put the kettle on she found Dave already in the kitchen.

'What time can we call the surgery for another appointment for Alfie? Sam looked at her watch.

'About ten minutes.'

'I'll do it!'

Sam walked away not knowing what to think. Dave always said he didn't know what to do when Alfie was ill. Now, here he was taking over from her, making her feel as if she was neglecting Alfie although she knew she wasn't. Annoyed, she went upstairs to find Alfie sitting up in bed.

She heard Dave on the phone downstairs. His voice raised. 'I want an appointment today. Now if possible. My son has been suffering enough, and I want a referral to the hospital. No!' he shouted, now does not mean tonight. Now, means now! We'll come in and wait. Make a note, Alfie James.' 'Take it easy, love, they do their best.'

'This has gone on long enough; you haven't pushed them. Now I am doing it. Get Alfie ready, I said we'll go in and wait. I will create again if we don't get seen quickly.'

Shocked, Sam woke Alfie up and got him showered and dressed, offering him cereal, touching her arm he shook his head.

'Throat still hurts? Alfie nodded. In answer she softened his cereal by showering it with lots of milk. They sat silently in the doctor's surgery waiting room, Dave looking uncomfortable in his seat. Alfie played with his Lego car looking flushed, and still rubbed his ear occasionally, but at least he wasn't crying anymore. The pain must have eased. Sam sat between the two hoping there would be no reason for Dave to start shouting again, having never seen him so annoyed and frustrated as this before.

The receptionist called 'Alfie James, they stood up, Dave grabbed Alfie's hand before Sam could and entered the doctor's room.

The doctor was already looking in Alfie's ear he also felt Alfie's glands. 'Say Ahhh!' He gently opened Alfie's mouth.

Alfie shrunk back in pain but managed to hold back the tears.

'Sore throat, swollen glands, earache are all signs of tonsillitis' he said. I'll give you some antibiotics.'

Standing up Dave shouted, 'NO!' They all jerked back; this has been going on long enough. Check your records. He's been in many times with the same or similar symptoms and he's had plenty of antibiotics it's not doing him any good. I want more done, much more! He's even been hospitalized and all you want to do is give him yet more antibiotics. I want, lots more done for my son!'

'Please calm down', said the doctor. This medication will help him and I will get a hospital appointment for the Ear, Nose and Throat department to examine him.

'How long will that take?' demanded Dave.

'I'll mark it urgent. It shouldn't be too long a wait.' Dave opened his mouth, but Alfie managed a 'Daddy! His voice sounded husky and strained.

'You're upsetting Alfie love', said Sam. Let's just get home.'

Dave strode out, annoyed. Sam, holding Alfie's hand rushed out behind him, checking that she had Alfie's prescription.

'It'll be fine love. We'll get an appointment soon and in the meantime these antibiotics will help him, I'm sure. They may even be stronger than the previous ones.

'He's had so much time off school', said Dave.

'He's only five, Dave, he'll do ok. In the meantime, I'll explain to the school and see if I can pick up something to keep him busy. He has got his school reading book I'll keep him interested in that as well. Lego keeps him busy and happy; you know how much he learns from that, but most of all he has to feel well enough to concentrate.'

'That's exactly what I mean', shouted Dave, as he walked off in a strop. Thankfully, Alfie had a restful night and Dave woke up nice and calm. Alfie heartily ate his breakfast of egg soldiers. Dave went to work in a good mood, much to Sam's relief. Alfie spent the day playing and resting. Sam was happy with this. He was a good child and was happy enough to entertain himself.

Chapter 13

While Alfie slept, Sam discretely got out the psychic books and found that the more she dived into them the more intrigued she became, wanting to learn and understand more about in-depth thoughts, feelings and ideas, so, began her practicing some of the exercises explained, such as those on meditations and visualizations. She chuckled to herself, for every time Alfie stirred the book was hidden behind a cushion. Reading and thinking was awakening Sam's brain and expanding her thought processes, with her mobile ringing, she remembered that it was on the kitchen worktop.

'Hello! Sam are you ok?'

'Was just engrossed with my reading.

'What are you reading mum?' Alfie was standing beside her; she was glad that she'd hidden the book.

'Can I say hi?' he whispered.

'Just a moment Carol'. Sam picked Alfie up and sat him on the kitchen top handing him her mobile.

'Hello Carol.'

'Hi Alfie! I can hear why you are at home again; you have a funny voice.' Alfie giggled, as Sam took away the mobile, put him down and watched him walk back to the couch.

'Hard to talk?' asked Carol.

'Not sure about pricked up ears.

What is happening with you?' Carol asked more about Alfie rather than speaking about herself

'Carol, can I call you later, after I've put Alfie to bed? Dave in not due home until late that gives us plenty of time to talk.'

'I'm sorry. I keep interfering with you and your family life.'

'No not at all.'

'Mummy!' Sam rushed around the corner to see Alfie being sick, trying to catch his sick in his hands.

'He's being sick Carol. I'll call you later.' Sam set about cleaning up after Alfie.

'Sorry mum, I couldn't catch it.' Sam gave Alfie a big hug, as she stripped off his messy clothes wrapping him in a nearby throw sat him on another seat while she quickly wiped down her sofa. Taking Alfie upstairs he was showered, given another dose of antibiotics, helped to clean his teeth and put into clean pyjamas. Tucked into bed, story time was too much as his heavy eyes soon closed. Wanting to be nearby Sam collected her book from downstairs and took it up with her, working out a place to hide it away from Dave never knowing how he was going to react to anything these days.

She got herself ready for bed, and in the warmth and comfort of their bedroom she rang Carol.

'Hello! Sam., I didn't expect to hear from you so soon.'

'Alfie's asleep already long story.

'Tell me.'

Sam told Carol all about Dave's behaviour at the doctor's and ended up by saying. 'I don't know if it's more to do with Alfie getting sick so often, or that he feels I'm not looking after him well enough.

'You're a great mum Sam. I'm sure Dave only intervened as he felt that the doctors weren't moving quickly enough and they needed a push'.

'Yes! That's exactly what he said.'

'There you go then', laughed Carol.

How are things with you?' Carol sighed.

'Not so good. One of the neighbours has given the police a description of the man Tanya was presumed to be living with. His fingerprints were not on file, so we have to assume that he has no criminal record. They are taking an artist impression of him around the neighbourhood. I dare say that is a long shot! I need to do something myself by getting things along quicker. Would you help me?'

'How?'

'I need to go back to the flat. Have a good look around. Check it out. See if anyone is willing to talk to me'.

'Of-course I'll help, but as you know I have Alfie at home at present'.

'I know'. Carol took a deep breath, but I have to do something, soon'. Carol said it helped her share her thoughts with Sam. Their conversation ended happily enough, but they both left with feelings of unfinished business to deal with.

Sam put her psychic book away and lay quietly in bed, allowing her mind to simply drift, and before she knew it Tanya appeared to her again. She shuddered in her bed, but the books she had been reading and learning from helped her to be brave by keeping an open mind. Once again, she saw Tanya's bright red lipstick and dark hair and then Tanya's lips moved, this time however, she was able to read them. Number 42 neighbour. Tanya was gone in a flash, as always. Looking everywhere, upstairs and down, there was no trace left of her. Grabbing a glass of water in the kitchen, she heard a click coming from the front door she was almost in a panic. Dave walked in.

'You waiting for me? He asked chirpily.

'Yeah! Of course,'. She smiled and winked at him. Her meeting with Tanya soon disappeared, as reality hit her when Dave tenderly and lovingly kissed her. He made her feel like the beautiful woman she believed she was.

'I've been waiting all day' he said. What were you doing wandering around in your silky night wear, anyway?'

'Getting a drink of water'.

'How's Alfie?' She smiled.

'I was going to check on him again but got side-tracked by a handsome man. Will you do it for

me?' They grinned at each other as Dave went into Alfie's room and Sam got her drink of water. They met on the landing again, kissed, and then headed back to bed. She heard Dave showering but soon drifted off to sleep, where she dreamt of Angels and bright magical places, where children played in the clouds, and where the face of a baby with twin-kling eyes, a snub nose and soft lips said,

'Hello! Mummy.'

Sam woke up to Dave whispering in her ear.

'Breakfast is served'. She stretched and blinked, trying to get out of her sleepy state, by which time her breakfast was laid on her bedside table. Dave soon returned carrying Alfie in a flying position as he laughed and giggled as his dad plonked him into bed beside Sam. Dave poured tea once Alfie was settled and handed him some toast. He nibbled slowly on it at first, but soon realized that he could bite and swallow without his throat hurting. He woofed the rest down quickly, washing it down with his milk. Dave ate his toast and drank his tea seated on the bed sideways. Sam found herself confused by her remembered dream and all that was presently happening around her.

'No breakfast for you? Asked Dave. She laughed as she picked crumbs from Alfie's pyjamas.

'I'm not fully awake yet. I'll have it in a minute'. They kissed. Alfie went 'yak!' They laughed.

Alfie improved remarkably quickly and was soon back at school by which time they had already received an appointment for him to see a specialist in the Children's hospital's ear, nose and throat department. The appointment was for only a week away, which pleased Dave no end.

In the meantime, Sam was pleased that she would have time to help Carol, so she rang her to let her know that she was free and arranged a day to visit Tanya's flat. Sam would collect Carol after she had dropped Alfie at school and they would drive to Tanya's together. Sam found Carol once again looking pale and drained, but who could blame her, she thought, going back and forth over these awful circumstances would more than drain anyone. Had that been me I would have probably had a nervous breakdown by now, she thought.

Carol directed Sam. 'This is Tanya's street.' They were driving past numbers in the 40's.

'Oh! God! Carol, I forgot to tell you. Tanya appeared to me again and she told me no.42 neighbour. I even managed to read her lips. I'm so sorry, I should have told you earlier, but with Alfie and everything... She drifted off.

Carol touched her arm. 'I understand', she said gently. Tanya's flat is no. 44. Sam looked shocked. That's where we will start, said Carol, firmly. They gave themselves a few moments to compose themselves, and then Sam followed Carol up the stairs to no. 42. Carol bravely rang the doorbell. Neither knew what to expect.

The door was answered by a kind elderly lady. 'Yes, Dears'.

'Sorry to trouble you Carol began. 'Did you happen to know the lady next door?' The lady looked them up and down, she seemed unable to make up her mind as to what she wanted to say or do.

'Why?' Her voice sounded much louder and stronger than a few moments earlier.

'I am her sister. I need some answers please. Can you help me?' Carol began to cry. Sam put her arm around her shoulders. 'Are you alone?' they both nodded. Come in, they were guided into the living room where she pointed to a small couch where they sat together, sitting opposite them she asked, so, you are Tanya's sister?'

'You knew her?'

'Yes, a lovely lady, but towards the end a very frightened one, I would say.' Carol sobbed quietly, but between the sobs she asked again, 'Can you help me?'

The lady went to the kitchen and soon they heard the click of the kettle being switched on. She returned and looked at Sam. 'I'm Sam, Carol's friend. Please there is so much we need help with.'

'Tea?' They both nodded in silence. She wandered into the kitchen and took some time in returning. She returned carrying a silver tray upon which was laid a tea pot, a sugar bowl, three sets of cups and saucers, three teaspoons, and a beautiful milk jug, the handles of which were shaped like Angel wings. She poured out the tea and after a minute or two and raised her hand sweeping it over the tray saying, 'Help yourselves.' They both helped themselves to milk and sugar. It seemed like an age before the lady spoke. 'I'm Queenie. I used to see Tanya coming and going. I would wave to her from the balcony she raised her eyes in its direction. She would smile and wave back, get into her car and go. I assumed she went off to work, left at 8.00 am, returned around 6.00 pm. I would see her return in the summer. In the winter I didn't go onto the balcony much. Other than that, we had no contact. After a while, at certain times she would bring a man home, he stayed. I would see her leave and he would be here. I could hear him moving about and would sometimes see him in our communal garden. They were no trouble at all. She took a deep breath and another sip of tea. Then, lots of other people started coming by, but only when he was around. Then the noise and confusion would start. Laughing, talking, swear-

ing, singing, shouting, and much more. It was never ending, it seemed. Other neighbours and I would knock and ask
them to quieten down. He would abuse us and threaten us.
Tanya never answered the door, only him. In the summer, I
stood on the balcony. It was then that I began noticing that
Tanya was often outside alone, looking sad, lost, and dis-
tressed much of the time. It seemed that she just wanted to
get away from the others, she would walk around the garden
alone, but if she went too far someone, anyone, would come
out and get her, taking her back to the flat. It was during one
of these times that we introduced ourselves. She was standing below my flat. I shouted, 'Hello Dear!' She smiled up at
me. 'Tanya' she said.

'Queenie'. Before I could finish my sentence, the man
came out, took her arm, and firmly led her back indoors.
That was when I began to get even more concerned for her.
He looked up, but I stepped back. I don't know if he saw me
or not.'

Sam and Carol sat and listened, it was as if Queenie
needed to talk about Tanya, there was so much emotion in
her words, all locked inside, it seemed, just waiting to be
allowed out. Queenie continued, 'Then suddenly it all went
quiet. No Tanya, no man, no car. I even went and knocked
on her door as I was so worried. Then I became frightened in
case the man came out and hurt me, but no, nothing, so I decided to phone the police. I phoned my local station and told
them that a young woman neighbour hadn't been seen for a
while. They asked my name; I was scared I gave them only
Tanya's address and flat number and hung up. It wasn't un-

til the next afternoon that the police showed up. They forced their way into the flat after banging on the door and shouting, Police! Police! Open up' a number of times. They must have called for an ambulance. Her eyes filled with tears. She shut them, but the tears still managed to escape running down her cheeks. She rubbed them away with her hand. I saw them take a body away.

'Sorry Dear', she said, looking at Carol. Carol broke down in tears. Sam managed to control hers as she held Carol tightly. Queenie went into the kitchen and switched on the kettle. She brought kitchen roll back with her. It helped mop up the many tears, which, by now, all three of them were shedding.

Carol finally managed to calm herself down. She took Queenie's hands and said, 'Thank you so much for caring about Tanya. I am so deeply hurt to hear all of this, but also so grateful for all that you did for her. It must have taken a lot of courage for you to knock on her door not knowing what would happen, then to phone the police.

'I have let her down, terribly,' said Carol.

'I liked her; I wish we could have been friends. Another cup of tea, Dears?

'No thank you', said Carol. She looked at Sam.

'We should go'

'Will you come again? I'd like us to be friends. Queenie chuckled, even though I am a lot older than the two of you'.

'Age is only a number', quoted Carol.

'Of-course we can be friends.

'Before you go, Dears, do you know if anyone was in Tanya's flat recently?'

'Yes, us. I have so much more to tell you, but can I ask one more question for now?' asked Carol.

'Of course.'

'Have the police questioned you and your neighbours recently?'

'Yes, they have. That's when I gave them the description of the man. I figured as nobody had been around here for so long, they would not return.

'Thank you so much, you have been a God send!' She felt compelled, so followed her instincts and kissed Queenie on the cheek. Queenie smiled back.

'What more can you tell me, dears?' 'Much, much, more Queenie, but I am drained now, and I am sure you are too. Can we come and see you again?'

'Of course, I'm always here apart from going shopping when I have to, and my walk around the garden like most of the other oldies. The young ones, she sighed, they come and go daily. I am so pleased that Tanya and I were able to share some moments of pleasantries, all be it for only short spells of time.' Sam stood up to leave as Carol followed suit, noticing Queenie's old telephone she asked. 'Would you like to give Carol your phone number? We can make arrangements to meet again. While writing her telephone number down, Queenie said, 'I'm always home, Dears'. They both hugged and thanked Queenie on the way out. Carol looked upwards as Sam pulled away. Queenie and Carol waved goodbye. Upon returning from the balcony Queenie said under her breath. 'I know something horrible must have happened to you, Tanya, Dear'. The empty cups and saucers on the table tinkled together in reply. Queenie was not afraid.

Chapter 14

Sam was feeling shattered herself, she didn't have any interest in her psychic books so, simply sat and stared into space thinking how scared and alone Carol must feel with all her problems, she admired her resourcefulness. I consider myself very lucky, she thought. I know Dave and I argue, but to me that only goes to show that we care for each other and Alfie, we only want what is best for us as a family.

She opened the local newspaper and glanced at the first few pages, her mind still wondering, as in shock she saw the face of the wanted man staring back at her. Queenie had given the police his description, she remembered, enabling them to ask the general public for help, she wondered if Carol had seen it, almost in response to her thoughts her mobile rang. She knew it must be Carol.

'Hello! Yes, I saw it. Maybe we will be lucky and someone will come forward, all thanks to Queenie', Carol said.

'I know, I thought that too, are you ok, asked Sam?'

'A bit shocked, but at least I am living in hope again. Can we go and see Queenie again? Day after tomorrow?

'Do you still want me to come with you? You two seem firm friends now!

'Of course, I want you to come with me!' Carol burst into tears and immediately said I'm sorry'.

'Don't be' Sam said. I was just sitting here thinking how brave you are to cope with all of this on your own, but check with Queenie, and of-course we'll go together. In the meantime, you take it as easy as you can, right? Carol was still crying as she clicked off her call with Sam.

Sam was also really upset and sat transfixed to the face in the newspaper again. It was going to be a long afternoon. How much worse must it be for Carol? Her having to be on her own day after day night after night. She wondered if she should ask her to stay over sometime, just for the company. She tried to imagine what Dave might say. He seemed in a better mood now that Alfie's health was being monitored more closely and decided to talk to him once Alfie was in bed. She could show him the newspaper article. Butter him up a bit by saying how lucky she was to have him by her side. What a great husband and father he is, then drop the question along the way. 'Can Carol stay with us for a while? We've got the room; she won't be any trouble. I'm sure she could do with some company.' She didn't get the chance, however, for after Sam had told him about going to Tanya's flat, about meeting Queenie, the whole story, he turned around and said.

'That's all very well love, but you don't know what this guy is like. Now that he has been flushed out, he might well come after people he feels may be helping the police. I'd keep well away from Tanya's flat. You have Alfie to consider, let alone me, the last thing we want is you getting hurt or worse.'

'I'll be careful,' she said very humbly. What she really wanted to do was scream at him. 'Get off your high horse! I am going to keep helping my friend no matter what you think or say.' Dave walked away. Oh! Well, she sighed. At lease it didn't lead to another argument and he didn't say not to go to Tanya's, he only suggested that I don't.

Sam sat and watched TV as Dave pottered about upstairs. She had no idea what he was doing, she didn't care as long as Alfie stayed asleep, he still had some catching up to do with his sleep pattern. The heavy footsteps of Dave arrived at the living room door. 'Cup of tea? he called out.

'Yes please, love.' They sat together drinking tea and watching television but it was obvious that they were both thinking their own thoughts. When their mugs were empty Dave collected them and took them into the kitchen. 'See you upstairs' he called, sticking his head in the opened living room door.

'OK' she replied, but took her time getting up there. Dave was sound asleep; she did not mind. She was tired herself.

Sam and Carol arranged to meet Queenie again, this time taking sandwiches and cake with them. Queenie welcomed them with open arms; the kettle was in much use. Carol told Queenie the in's and out of Tanya's sad departure and there were moments of laughter around the sadness. Their friendship seemed to blossom and grow and soon Sam was telling Queenie all about her family as well. Time flew away too quickly once again.

After being at Queenie's they went back to their own homes. Sam tidied around a bit and paid a quick visit to the supermarket, then going directly onto the school, where once again Alfie stood with his teacher.

'He's been unwell again', she said.

'We have an appointment to see a specialist next week Sam said in reply. I will inform the school administration.' Smiling, the teacher handed Alfie over to Sam she wiped her hand on her skirt as Alfie had left her hand as sweaty as his own. Carrying him to the car, he did not look well at all. On the drive home she glanced back at him. He was sniffing and beginning to cough.

Once indoors she showered him and put him into his pyjamas. He looked miserable and didn't want to eat. Knowing that he needed lots of fluid, especially when ill, she gave him some fresh orange juice in his favourite plastic glass with a straw. He settled himself in front of the television with Sam sitting beside him but soon climbed onto her lap and in no time fell asleep. The course of antibiotics was completed, she'd have to give him a dose of Calpol at bedtime. She dozed off, but woke with a start when Dave walked in. She had no idea what the time was. He looked at them. 'Well!' he said. Both sound asleep'. At first Sam did not know if he was joking or not, but then he smiled.

'I'm sorry, she said, 'I'll get tea started'.

'Relax. I'll get out of this stuffy suite and join you. We'll get a takeaway later, ok? She smiled, still feeling tired, her eyes were already shutting as Dave walked away. Upon his return Alfie stirred. Opening one eye he said, 'Hello! Daddy'. Dave smiled, ruffling his hair.

'Glad that appointment is next week Dave said. Got to

get this sorted. I'll check the calendar. I'll get time off work and go with you.' Sam took his hand.

'Thanks!' What else could she say knowing that something had to be done to help Alfie.

'Would you tuck Alfie in bed for me? I'll love a shower; I feel all hot from him.' Dave read to Alfie as Sam showered.

During the week Sam and Dave talked to Alfie about him seeing, what they called a special doctor at the hospital and in time he got used to the idea. Dave was accompanying them and this pleased Alfie.

Sam had a quick call from Carol to let her know that Detective Campbell had been in touch. He informed her they had received some good results from their piece in the local newspapers. Members of the public had come forward with information, based on this they were making further inquiries.

'We are daein our best, hen' he said. Carol could not help but smile to herself at his expression and accent. Sam noticed that Carol's voice seemed lighter. She told Sam that she felt as if things were moving forward at last. Sam did not say anything but hoped that Carol would not be let down in any way.

Alfie seemed to recover from his bout of illness and was soon back at school. Sam was pleased, she wanted him to be and feel normal again before seeing the specialist. When the day of his appointment arrived Alfie was pain free, no swollen glands, no raised temperature or any other health problems. He was however a bag of nerves, which made her feel very nervous also. They were both pleased that Dave was going with them.

The James family sat in the waiting room of the hospital in the Ear, Nose and Throat Department. Their name was soon called and a nurse led them in to see the Specialist. He introduced himself to Dave and Sam as Dr. Brown and bent down to shake hands with Alfie. As Alfie shook hands with him, he looked up at his mummy and daddy, looking very proud and grown up. It didn't stop there, for the doctor spoke directly to Alfie. 'You know you have been feeling very poorly, well I am here to help you feel better, but you must allow me to give you a good check-up first, ok?' Alfie nodded very firmly. He took Alfie's hand and led him into the examination room, while calling out. 'Would mummy and daddy like to come along too?' Smiling in amusement they followed the doctor. They were amazed how wonderful he was with Alfie, and how quickly he had put him at ease. They stood and watched as he helped Alfie onto the high bed saying, 'jump up! Alfie giggled and obliged. Can I look in your mouth?' He shone his touch in. He felt Alfie's glands and looked into his ears he did some other checks also. Alfie seemed relaxed and happy. Everything seemed to be completed quickly and efficiently. The doctor helped Alfie down and said. 'We have some toys next door. Would you like to go and play with them? While I talk to your mummy and daddy'. The nurse appeared; Alfie held her hand as they left the room.

The specialist began to explain. 'From checking Alfie over, and studying his records, it seems that he has a problem with both his tonsils and adenoids. These are the first part of the immune system used in the protection of bacterial infections but can sometimes become infected themselves. The bacteria and viruses enter through the mouth and nose, hence the trouble with Alfie's throat so often, which in turn leads to airway problems and more, hence the vast amount of antibiotics' having been administered to Alfie over a short space of time. Normally we don't intervene at such an early age, but in Alfie's case we now know that the answer is in performing a tonsillectomy and adenoidectomy.

'What?

'Let me explain Mrs. James, we would like to remover Alfie's Tonsils and Adenoids. It is an operation which we have done many times. It would stop any reoccurring problems and is really the best result for Alfie.

'If it's for Alfie's wellbeing then it must be done', said Dave, regaining his composure after being told that an operation would be involved. Sam nodded in agreement. 'You will be guided on the day, but generally the child would be put to sleep. The whole operation process will take around half an hour and then he will go into the recovery room and be closely monitored. He will probably feel dizzy and sleepy at first, but that's normal and he will feel uncomfortable for a while, be in pain, and be given painkillers. He will go home and rest, at most for two weeks, but all being well he should be able to return to school after ten days'

Sam phoned Carol the following day to give her an update on how Alfie's appointment went, and his need for the operation. They agreed to meet for a coffee early the following week, so did not speak for too long.

Sam meanwhile spent more of her free time with her books and now even began to look up information on the Internet regarding the Spiritual and Physic part of her evolving life. She looked into circle development which involved sitting in a group and learning from a well-established mediums', wondering if that was a good starting point for her although still not understanding how all these connections and emotions she was experienced worked, or if she even possessed any type of ability, for other than Tanya appearing to her, there was nothing else. There were so many questions that she decided to talk to Carol about it when they next met.

Carol listened, or maybe only half listened, for Sam found her responds to be rather vague. She wondered why, until Carol eventually told her the truth of how she was feeling and why she didn't want to talk to her about it.

'I know that you are really wrapped up in all of this Sam, but please understand that all I can think about right now is putting Tanya's soul to rest, maybe we should just visit the Spiritualist church where you can still watch, listen and learn. I don't mean to interfere in your family life, but

from what you have told me Dave's not impressed with your new interest. How are you going to handle that?'

Sam was getting more and more frustrated and annoyed while listening to Carol's speech.

'If it wasn't for your sister, I wouldn't be in this predicament! Now that I've done all that is necessary for you, you want to leave me high and dry, when all I am looking for is a bit of guidance and advice from you. This is the second time you have taken what I had to give, but don't want to give anything back, I shan't wait for a third time!' Sam got up and left. Carol sat in shock. By the time everything registered with her, Sam was long gone.

The two women sat in their own homes both trying to figure out what had happened, their minds remembering a jumble of words said in haste. Yet neither wanted to be the first to apologize. Dave came home asking if an appointment had arrived for Alfie. Sam was still in a bad mood but tried not to let it show. 'Not yet love', she said in as gentle a voice as she could muster.

Chapter 15

In the meantime, Carol and Sam stayed apart, Sam hoping that Alfie's hospital day would arrive soon, wanting her own life to move forward. As if her wish came true, the next day Alfie's appointment arrived. It was for the end of the week. Dave was pleased too, and they set about explaining to Alfie that once this operation was done, he would feel much better. They hoped he wouldn't get ill at this late stage.

Sam didn't bother to let Carol know, but she did take her advice however, and having made enquiries about daytime Spiritual services, she took herself along to one, to prove that she could work out for herself where her next steps would lead regarding her Spiritual development and if that would be her best move. At the end of the service Sam hung around but she wasn't sure who to talk to or what to say. In the end the Church leader came over to her.

'Are you ok? 'Can I help you?

Sam hesitated, and then in one quick breath said.

'I'm interested in learning more. I read about joining a circle, is there one held here?'

The lady seemed taken back but said. 'One is due to start soon. Shall I get the medium running the group to contact you?'

'That would be most helpful' said Sam, hoping that her words hadn't sounded too formal.

Her details were added to the list of interested people, although she did not hear any more for a while.

In a way Sam was pleased, for first, she wanted Alfie's operation to be a success, with him making a complete recovery and returning to school. Only then would she have the space and time to join this circle. Whatever that was!

Alfie was naturally nervous on the day, but everything moved very quickly and soon he was in the operating theatre. Sam and Dave stayed with him until he was totally under sedation and then went into the waiting room. Dave busied himself pacing the room and looking at his watch as in what seemed forever, the surgeon appeared.

'Alfie has done great! he said. The nurse will take you in to visit him soon'.

'Thank you' they said in unison. He was already gone. Sam and Dave hugged in relief.

Alfie was lying in bed looking groggy. They both walked to either side of the bed and took a hand. Alfie knew they were there. Opening his eyes, he smiled at them, but soon drifted off back to sleep. Luckily, as planned, he was soon home, resting, and getting his strength and voice back. As he progressed, he was playing with his Lego and playing board games with Sam. It was during one of these times that he suddenly said to Sam.

'Mummy, I shall call you Mum now, as I am a big brave boy and I will call daddy, Dad. My friends at school have been doing that for ages..

'Ok Alfie love, she said. You really have been a big, brave, boy.' He seemed to stop and think for a while.

'What are you thinking about?' she asked. Is it about the little girl you liked in the hospital?'

'No! Carol. Why has Carol not come to see me? I like her.' Sam was taken aback.

'She must think I'm very busy with you and we are, aren't we? We are having lots of fun, too.'

'We can do the same with Carol here. Play these games with her, he pointed to the toys scattered around him on the couch. Anyway, he continued, I have something to tell her, a message.'

'What?' said Sam. Tell me.'

'I need to see Carol!' demanded Alfie.

'Don't talk to me like that young man! It is nice to hear you, but not in that tone of voice.

'I have to talk to Carol', he said again, in his normal voice as he grabbed his Lego and went upstairs.

Sam sat and thought for a while.

Alfie was just out of hospital, she didn't want him upset, but she did feel his behaviour was more than just rude, it was also very strange. What did he mean about having to see Carol? Having a message for her? That can only amount to Tanya having appeared to him again, that was concerning, the beginning of her worries about Alfie's sanity and safety had just begun.

Dave's warnings about Carol's influence were beginning to ring in her ears. Worrying, she went upstairs to check on Alfie. He was sound asleep, breathing easily and gently, with his Lego on his pillow beside him. She wondered if she should phone Carol, or should she try to talk to Alfie again? Perhaps this time she'll use a gentler manner, but then, quickly became annoyed again as she thought about how adamant Alfie was in wanting to talk to Carol directly. She picked up her mobile scanning it for Carol's number but quickly changed her mind, deciding to try to talk to Alfie first.

The following morning, she was cooking breakfast as Dave walked in. 'Nice! He said, breathing in the aroma of bacon. They kissed good morning.

'Sit and enjoy.' She placed his plate before him, then pouring his coffee.

'Alfie is on the mend it's nice to see him getting back to normal.'

'Yes', Sam said.

Dave looked at her. 'Are you ok?'

She smiled 'Of course'.

'Thought you'd have more to say about Alfie, that's all.'

'He's doing well. Still tired but ok, her few words surprised him, but he said nothing. Finishing breakfast, he headed for the door.

He was just about to open it when he heard 'Dad!' Turning around Alfie was standing at the top of the stairs, carrying him down Dave stood him in the kitchen.

'Got to go Son' he said, ruffling Alfie's hair, waving goodbye as he left.

'Cereal?'

'Yes please', Alfie smiled, but noticed that his mother hadn't returned the smile, but she had given him his favourite cereal. Sam watched Alfie. No more sore throat or swallowing problems. Nothing. She was once again pleased, relieved and grateful. Alfie ate heartily. Having taken a gulp of milk and drank it he asked.

'Is Carol coming 'round?' Sam tried to keep calm.

'Why?'

'I have to speak to her'.

'Can you tell me what about? She tried hard to make her voice sound natural and calm, but inside her emotions was running wild. Alfie looked at her, white moisture of milk on his upper lip. He looked cute and funny. Normally Sam would have laughed and made Alfie laugh too, but at that moment she just wanted Alfie to talk to her.

I'll have to phone Carol. I haven't spoken to her in a while. I was too worried about you.' Alfie smiled.

'Can I call her?'

'We'll see what happens later in the day,' said Sam. Can't you tell me about her message first, and then we can phone her? Alfie looked annoyed.

'The message is for Carol mum'.

'Whom from?' Alfie gulped.

'Can I leave the table, please?' Sam had become increasingly annoyed, now she spoke to Alfie firmly, but without raising her voice.

'You are five years old Alfie. I'm your mum. I have a right to know what is happening to you.'

Glaring at Sam Alfie said. 'Mum!' Tanya told me that you and Carol have not been getting along very well. I just want to bring both of you together again. He ran over and gave her a huge hug. I love you mum, but I like Carol too.'

She held him tight and close. 'Ok, let's get ourselves ready then we'll give her a ring.' Sam was relieved. She helped Alfie have his shower. He dressed himself, tee shirt on back to front. Sam got herself ready, after which they headed downstairs and she phoned Carol.

'Sorry for the miss understandings'.

'Me too', said Carol.

'I have someone here who wants to speak to you.

'Hello!' said Alfie.

'You sound good,' said Carol.

Alfie giggled.

'Mum says, 'do you want to come over and have lunch with us later?

'She said yes', Alfie told Sam, as Sam took her mobile back from him.

'See you soon Carol.' Alfie had mended their fractured friendship.

Sam checked her fridge; it was practically empty.

'We have to go shopping, love. Let's get your shirt on the right way. Arms up.' Alfie obliged and they were soon on their way to the supermarket. They shopped, laughed and had fun along the way. There was even an ice cream to be had. Sam was glad they were soon having fun again; however, she did remind Alfie that he could talk to her about anything, for she, as his mum, always needed to know that he was fine and that nothing was worrying or frightening him.

Alfie listened patiently. An innocent look on his face. His quiet response was a 'Yes mum.'

Alfie played with his toys while Sam prepared lunch and both waited for Carol to arrive. She appeared with flowers for Sam and this time a Lego book for Alfie. The women had their customary hug and Alfie got a tight squeeze from Carol.

They were eating and drinking when Alfie said. 'Carol, Tanya came to see me again.' Carol stopped chewing. She said that everything is going to be sorted now and she is feeling more at rest. What does that mean, at rest?'

Sam and Carol looked at each other. 'It means that she can relax said Carol. But Alfie darling you do know that she is not here, she lives in another world and our two worlds only meet sometimes, right?' This was Sam's opportunity. 'Does it frighten you when Tanya comes into our world and talks to you?'

'No mum, she is kind and gentle and tells me things then goes away again, that's all.'

'Do you know that she is dead, love?' Sam asked nervously.

'Yes mum. She comes to me because I can see and hear her. If I can help people like I have helped Carol and Tanya I might want to do that when I grow up. I don't know yet.' Carol and Sam listened to Alfie, amazed at him taking everything in his stride at such a tender age. Sam admired him remembering how she would panic when Tanya first began appearing to her. Alfie was her main concern and he was obviously happy and safe in Tanya's company. Alfie kept eating when he wasn't talking, where-as Sam and Carol sat dumb-founded.

Sam wanted to get more information from Alfie while she had the chance. 'Have you ever told anyone about Tanya? Would you, love?'

'No said Alfie in his very firm voice again. My friends and I talked about ghosts at Halloween time. They think that Ghosts and Spirits are only pretend but they are still frightened by them so I won't tell anyone, expect for those who I have messages for, that's why I only wanted to tell Carol myself. He looked at Sam firmly saying, I think it is the right thing to do.' Sam smiled, giving Alfie a cuddle.

'I understand but remember that I am here to listen to you, about anything. That is part of my mum job as well.' Sam was very proud to think that Alfie was already honest and discreet; she hoped that he would always remain the same.

Carol sat taking in the conversation. 'If Tanya says all will be well, I believe her, but I have heard nothing from Detective Campbell in what seems like ages.'

Can I be excused' asked Alfie?'

'Before you go love. From what you've said I guess you haven't told Daddy',

'Dad', interrupted Alfie.

Sam smiled, 'About your second visit from Tanya?'

'No mum, and I hope you don't tell him either, it only makes you fight'.

'You may leave the table my very grown-up son', she said.

'Come here!' said Carol, picking Alfie up then sitting him

on her lap. Putting both arms around his body she cuddled him tightly rubbing her chin on the top of his head. 'That tickles!' he laughed.

'I wanted to show you have much I love you and to thank you for all your help.'

'That's alright', he said, while wriggling off Carol's lap and then running off.

'Thank you too, she said to Sam for having such an adorable son. He will grow up to be a real helper in life, and I hope we will have no more arguments about mediumship and the like.'

'I can't guarantee that, but I have actually put my name down to sit in circle.

'Then it's time I told you my story said Carol, but right now I would like to spend some time with Alfie if that is alright with you.'

'You play. I'll tidy and clear up.'

Carol joined Alfie on the carpet with his Lego. When Carol was leaving, she said 'let's meet at mine next time, coffee and lunch perhaps?'

'Yes, we'll make that a date,' laughed Sam.

'You get Alfie back to school and make sure he is alright'.

'Yeah! I'm going to talk to him, maybe get him back tomorrow, and break him in gently. They hugged and said goodbye. Poor Alfie getting unintentionally squashed as he stood between them. They both waved Carol off at the front door.

Chapter 16

It was a happy evening at home having dinner and spending time with Dave. They both told him about Carol's visit leaving out the bits they choose to. Sam approached Alfie about returning to school he was more than happy to return the following morning.

With Alfie in bed Dave sloped off to the kitchen returning with a glass of wine for Sam and a beer for himself. 'I'm a clever boy too, he said. Sam looked at him surprised. I'm a boss now. I have been promoted' he said, grinning ear to ear. I have three people to organize and keep in line. Well worth it though, big pay rise included. We can afford much more now Sam. Bigger and newer cars, clothes, even moving to a new house in a better area. Whatever you and Alfie want Sam, isn't that great?' Sam didn't want to burst his bubble, but it really wasn't what she wanted, and she thought that Alfie would feel the same. Sam kissed him. 'Congratulations! but I really don't want anything more, I am fine as I am.'

'We'll talk some more once we've told Alfie, for now let us celebrate, just the two of us.' Sam went along with Dave but she could sense trouble brewing.

Dave already began getting home later and later. He said it was the changeover period and soon he would delegate and be home early. That was the plan, but Sam suspected that would never happen. Dave's working hours grew even longer. Alfie complained to him that he was never home in time for dinner or to put him to bed.

'We can do lots of things over the weekends Alfie. How about we go to the park now?'

Sam was in the middle of sorting washing, she told them to go ahead, that she would catch up.

'Take your mobile,' she said to Dave. 'We don't want to miss each other in the park.' She took her time and was very tempted to take out her psychic books but resisted. It did serve to remind her however that she hadn't heard from the Spiritualist Church about the commencing of a new circle. She also noted that Carol and she hadn't been to the Church and that there were no more visits from Tanya. Her mind was awash with thoughts of the why's and what for, so a trip to the park was what she needed to blow away the cobwebs.

Dave and Alfie were having fun kicking around a football as Alfie's bike lay nearby. She came into ear shot as Dave said. 'Would you like a new bike, Alfie?' Sam stopped. No! She thought; he doesn't ask for much, don't entice him to want more, there's no need.

Alfie looked seriously at Dave. 'Don't need one'. Phew! Sam was happy, she nearly yelled out well done love, but smiled happily to herself instead.

Dave continued. 'You've had this one for ages.'

'But I like it and it still fits my size.' Dave looked disappointed as Sam called Alfie's name and ran over to them.

With Sam's arrival the talk of the bike ended. Sam gave Dave a hug.

'You two look like you were having fun'.

'Smashing!' said Alfie. Dave only looked on.

The family returned home and at once Sam began preparing their meal. Dave seemed restless.

'What's wrong love?' asked Sam.

'Why is no one else excited about my new job? Why is it when I offer you nice things you both turn it down?'

Sam left the spuds to boil and went over to Dave. 'Because we love you and we want you here with us. I keep telling you Alfie and I don't need anything. You provide for us more than adequately, that's why I don't need to work. Did you have a choice in accepting this promotion? We could have talked about it first.'

'I can make my own decisions, Dave flared back. Now you are trying to tell me that I made the wrong one!' He stormed off and bumped into Alfie at the bottom of the stairs. Alfie innocently laughed. He glared at him, 'Now you are laughing at me too, fine family I've turned out to have.'

Alfie raced over to Sam. 'Mum, he said. 'Have you and Dad been fighting again?' He sat at the table and cried. Sam was at the point of tears too, but dinner had to be cooked and eaten.

Dave returned to find Alfie crying while Sam drained the potatoes. He went over to Alfie and ruffled his hair. 'Love you son' he said. Alfie looked at him through tear-stained eyes. Sam asked Alfie to go and wash his hands. To Sam's' surprise father and son did it together. The family sat down to eat. It was a quiet meal, each thinking their own thoughts. The rest of the evening was subdued, but they both got Alfie ready and into bed. Sam dreaded how the rest of their evening may go, but her mobile rang.

'Hi Sam. Can you talk?' Sam looked at Dave who shrugged his shoulders in reply. Sam walked away to talk in private. Dave was sitting, whiskey in hand as Sam apologised for the interruption. Sam spoke to Carol quickly. Her insight told her that Carol knew that something was amiss.

Upon her return Dave moaned. 'You tell me you don't get enough time with me, then when I am here you are not, how do you think that makes me feel? Un-wanted! That's how. I don't get calls about work nor any other calls do I? You seem to pick out the bad parts of my job but dismiss the good. I simply don't know what to think anymore.' She could tell by Dave's voice he was angry, but in a roundabout way she could also identify with what he was saying. This made her battle with her own thoughts and emotions. Dave was right, he did not get work calls at home, but he did get his nights out with friends. It was not all work and no play as he was making it appear.

'Sorry!' she said, she wasn't even sure what about, but she didn't like these arguments that kept flaring up, now even upsetting Alfie and bringing him to tears.

Dave and Sam sat together on the couch.

'Sorry' said Dave. Don't know what is happening to us and why, but I don't like it.'

'Me neither' sighed Sam, their conversation ended, but they continued to sit beside each other. Slowly their hands moved nearer, soon they were holding hands and kissing. Happily, they went to bed as in no time Dave fell asleep. Sam however, laid thinking about the ebbs and flows accruing within their marriage, a marriage which was stable until Tanya's ghostly appearance invaded their lives, now casting huge waves of uncertainty. Dave's new job was an easy bone to pick at, but was her guilt of hiding things from Dave playing its part too? With too many thoughts crowding her mind she finally fell into a restless sleep.

The following morning Dave woke her with a cup of coffee.

'No cooked breakfast today', he quipped. Have to leave early, not sure if you had set your alarm, wouldn't want Alfie to be late for school'. He pecked her on the cheek before she even had the chance to wake up properly checking her alarm clock there was plenty of time. No! She thought, now he's even leaving early for work. What the hell was I feeling guilty about last night? She drank her coffee and decided to get up. Having a shower made her feel better, refreshed in body and mind.

It was while in the kitchen drinking a glass of fresh orange that she noticed a few sheets of paper laying on one of the kitchen tops, walking over, she picked them up. Turning them over she realized that they were flyers from housing agencies. Open mouthed she looked at the pictures and scan read some of the details, interrupted by tiny footsteps they were hurriedly put away into a drawer.

'Alfie love.'

'Mum! Where's dad?'

'Gone to work'. She glanced at the clock, she was glad that she was ready, as time had marched on, and in Dave's words 'she wouldn't want Alfie late for school' served as a reminder of where Dave's attitude lay. Her mind was all over the place again. I've just spoken to him about making decisions alone, now, he's done it again and simply expects me to go along with it, she thought. She suddenly realized that Alfie was staring at her.

'You ok mum? You look angry again.'

She forced a smile.

'Just thinking too much love. Let's get you sorted and ready for school.'

They chatted on the drive, about Lego of course, but she wanted to make sure that Alfie was fine and not dwelling on her angry face. He wasn't.

Sam took time out for herself before going to Carol's for coffee and lunch. She had a quick walk around the park enjoying the bright autumn morning. The trees were changing colour, it was beautiful. It took her mind away from Dave for a while. There were patches of leaves lying on the ground. Sam walked through them, dragging her feet enjoying the sound of rustling leaves. Sadness suddenly overtook her as she thought of her American friend. Patsy loved watching the change of seasons in England, being a Californian girl, autumn, the fall, as she would say was her favourite season. Walking through fallen leaves was what these two friends enjoyed doing together. Sometimes, if it was a cold day, they would both get red and runny noses and would laugh at the sight of each other as they scrambled to find tissues. This is terrible she thought. I'll be a nervous wreck by the time I get to Carol's, maybe I should cancel, but instead she went home, washed her face, put on a bit of lippy, and was good to go!

They hugged as Sam entered. 'Kettle's on, tea or coffee?'

'Coffee thanks'. When it was ready Carol placed their hot drinks on a little table between them. Excitedly Carol told Sam. 'I finally saw Tanya although there was no communication, only her quick appearance and disappearance. It was just enough to let me know that she in now safe and settled. Her body is back in the ground, her soul is at peace, we can all move on, except. I haven't heard any news from Detective Campbell. I intend giving him a ring soon.' They talked and laughed over lunch, all very false on Sam's part until she could no longer pretend.

'I hope you don't mind, she said to Carol, but I need to go home and do a few chores. We were out at the park with Alfie yesterday, which was true, lost a bit of time there,' but, Carol wasn't told that she did stop indoors and do some other chores, she surprised herself at how good she was becoming at only saying what she wished to and hiding the rest, thanks to the practice she was getting with behaving like that with Dave.

Sam got home but felt uncomfortable the minute she stepped through the door but did not understand why. The truth was that her intuition was getting stronger and she was picking up on negative vibrations created due to her constant arguments with Dave. This was all part of her psychic and spiritual growth taking place within herself but was as yet unknown to her. Looking at her books she realized that their due day had sneaked up on her, giving her the opportunity to get out the house for longer while renewing her books, and having a brose around the library.

Upon returning home she had quickly fallen asleep on the couch but was disturbed by the tune of her mobile ringing. It was a call from Jade, the medium.

'Sam, the circle is due to begin next week. I will be sending out emails with dates and times as I feel people remember better if it is written down, especially at the beginning.'

'You don't have my email address,' retorted Sam.

'I would have realized that and used the other option I had.' She could swear that she heard Jade add a 'tut' to the end of her sentence. She wondered why it was that every side she turned recently she seemed to be upsetting people.

'OK, sorry!' said Sam.

'Shall I put you down as a starter now that I have spoken to you?'

'Yes. Can you give me the dates and times?'

Jade answered, 'I was just about to.' Was that another tut I heard, wondered Sam. She scribbled the information down and thanked Jade. She saw this as a bad start in her association with her and could only hope that their connection would improve.

Sam finally began to feel more at ease in the house for which she was most grateful. She and Alfie stopped expecting Dave home in time for dinner. Alfie missed him at bedtime, but he was promised that they would do something special every weekend to make up for it. There was plenty they hadn't seen and done in their area and now was the time to start having more adventures with Alfie.

Just to show a bit of interest in Dave's work Sam asked him from time to time how things were going. His usual reply was 'fine'. No details, no co-worker names, no information at all ever came forward. She once said to him after he'd said fine, yet again.

'Anyone would think you were in the secret service'. Dave didn't see the funny side and slyly remarked that they were a creative company, always inventing something new, their products were a secret until they arrived on the market. Which of-course is my job, to make sure the products are advertised and sold, I am a salesman.'

'I know love, I was only joking as you never say anything else rather than fine, the whole conversation went totally over Dave's head.

One Saturday morning while having breakfast Dave said. 'How about we go into town. Go into the Mall and spend some money.

Alfie's eyes got as bit as saucers as he looked at his dad.

'The Mall, anything we want?' asked Alfie.

'Hooked!' said Dave and winked at Sam. He looked so happy she simply had to agree.

'Well Alfie if your dad wants to spend some of his hard-earned money on us, who are we to say no?' Dave couldn't stop smiling as they got ready to go out.

'Dave went over to Sam and said. 'Do you think Carol would like to come along?' Sam smiled.

'I can but ask'. Carol was hesitant, speaking of it being

their family time, so she didn't want to interrupt, get in the way.

Alfie sorted that out by shouting.

'Come with us Carol, we all want you to', they agreed that it would be fun if they all went together, so they collected Carol from her house. Alfie had asked if he could get Carol and so he walked up the stairs and rapped on her front door with his knuckles. The doorbell was too high for him to reach. He stretched out his hand to her. Holding hands, they walked together and got into Dave's car. When Sam turned around to speak to Carol, she noticed that Carol's hand was on the middle hand rest with Alfie's on top of hers. Finding that image so cute, she forgot what she was going to say. Turning to the front and smiling at Dave he realized that something different was going on. Glancing into his rear-view mirror he saw what Sam was referring to; they both smiled and nodded in amusement.

The Mall was a wild success. After looking around for a while they all sat down to food and drink after which Dave suggested they part company.

'Buy something for both of you.' He looked at Carol and blushed.

Carol was about to protest when Sam jumped in and said.

'It's ok Carol. He just wants to share some of his extra pay cheque with everyone. Carol looked at both of them and said, Thank you'.

Dave took Alfie's hand from Sam saying, 'We're going this way' and they were gone.

'Come on Carol, let's spend some money.' Under much duress Carol agreed, she ended up buying a pair of leather gloves, while Sam bought a leather jacket, there was plenty of money remaining. They had agreed to meet by a particular shop and so were waiting when Dave and Alfie arrived with lots of bags.

'It's like Christmas', shouted Alfie as he saw them, he had two matching bags and put the ones he was carrying on the floor, then handed both Carol and Sam a gift bag each.

'Help!' shouted Dave as he handed a few smaller bags back to Alfie. They all headed for the car laughing and talking together.

The women sat with their gift bags on their laps while the others were in the car boot. Alfie looked so happy that Sam thought he might just burst.

Back home Alfie took all his presents out of the bags. He spread them all over the floor showing everyone what he had bought. Amongst the pile was a new football, books, pencils, board and electronic games, a real variety of toys.

'This is for dad he said proudly, it's a drone.' Sam in pretence wagged a finger at him, as if telling him off.

'Alfie bought it for me, I couldn't say no.' They all laughed. From his place on the carpet Alfie shouted. 'Open yours' looking at Sam and Carol. It's from dad and me, but I choose them.'

'He has good taste' Dave said, just like his father.' Inside each presentation bag was a box containing silver, four charmed bracelets.

Alfie went to Dave who gave him two small envelopes.

Dave peeped into one, bent down and whispered to him. Alfie handed that envelope to Carol and the other to Sam. They each took their surprise out of their envelopes at the same time. A sparkly charm letter S and a sparkly charm letter C. Sam went over and kissed Dave, rather more tenderly than she intended to. Alfie said his usual 'Yak!' As Carol blushed.

When they moved apart Carol said. 'Thank you, Dave thank you to all of you. I've had a wonderful day.' She cuddled Alfie.

'I don't hear you going yak! Now teased Sam.

Alfie's reply was, 'MUM!'

They asked Carol to stay the night.

'Let's see what I have to cook for dinner.'

'Carol do stay said Dave. We can get a takeaway love, don't worry about cooking.'

'That would make a nice end to the day,' said Sam.

'Stay! Stay!' Alfie called out going over to Carol, noticing that Sam and Dave had left the room.

Sam returned saying, 'Can we make another deal?'

'What deal, asked Carol?

'After dinner, if you decide to stay it means that Dave and I can go out for a while, we'd like that.'

Alfie got excited again. 'Say yes, Carol, we'll have lots of fun with my new toys.

'OK' said Carol. I'll give in again.' They all laughed. After their Indian take away Carol insisted that she cleans up so as Dave and her could get out.

'My mobile is on if you need us', Sam said to carol.

She gave Alfie a stern look, 'Be good now', she said.

'We'll be fine and thank you both again for this special day.'

'We won't be too long', said Dave, ruffling Alfie's hair and also saying, 'Be good' to him.

Dave drove until they came to a high spot. They got out of the car admiring the beautiful bright lights of the city below hand in hand they enjoyed the walk, until they came to a bench. They sat together, still looking below them. It felt as if they were sitting on top of the world!

Sam sighed. 'This is so beautiful, so romantic.' Dave squished her hand. She didn't want this night to get serious, but her instincts told her that this was the best time for talking. 'I love you,' she spoke gently and softly into Dave's ear. You and Alfie are everything to me, but I need to be myself too, please listen to me Dave'.

Dave could hear the emotion in Sam's voice, he knew this was important. 'I am listening' he said, holding her hand even tighter.

'I have been keeping things from you and I can't do it anymore, it makes me feel guilty and just horrible. Yet, I don't want to have any more disagreements. I want you to try to understand me, to help me to find my way, find the path I need to take. Dave kissed her on the cheek. 'That's encouraging, she said, 'thank you. I have to tell you that Tanya did not appear to Alfie only on one occasion, but twice. She felt Dave stiffen up. Please, she said, this is very difficult for me. She continued. In spite of her appearances no harm has come to either one of us, and now I just know it won't, but because of those experiences I have to learn more about my spiritual path, my psychic path, for I believe it is all interrelated. If anything, changes, I promise I will pull out.

'Pull out of what?' asked Dave.

'I want to join a group where you learn how to develop your psychic gifts and in time learn to communicate with those in Spirt, like Tanya, and those gifts can be used to help other people in a good way. We've learnt that for ourselves, haven't we? I was able to help Carol, but because I didn't understand what was happening to me, we had so many problems, I don't want that to happen to others. I want you to know, love, so I don't have to hide anything from you ever again. I've been reading and practicing some psychic exercises from books borrowed from the library.' Sam gave another big sigh. Well, it's all out in the open now, that's where it should be. There are probably bits and pieces I have left out unintentionally, but I couldn't live with not talking to you about any and everything. I have always been that way with you'. Dave lifted his arm placing it around Sam's shoulder. Gently he pulled her into him. She rested her head on his chest, both sitting in silence, thinking.

After a while Dave spoke. 'I don't know much about what you speak of, but I do know, or rather feel that you have been different. Perhaps you are keeping part of yourself from me has made me feel less of a part of you. I love you and will help you in any way I can and that includes listening and talking to you just as we have tonight.'

'Thank you, that's all I ask for', she said. They kissed again.

'Our seal of approval, Dave said. We will always make

a point of listening and talking to each other more openly, more often, and more honestly from now on.'

'That includes no hidden house buying agendas.' Sam pretended to scold.

'Deal, next time I want to move, we'll look at houses together.'

'There you go again. I don't want to move', said Sam, almost in tears, thinking of the time and effort she'd spent in talking to him only a moment ago.'

'It's ok love, I've learnt my lesson. I thought about how selfish I have been. You and Alfie have to feel comfortable wherever we are. We should have a choice and come to a family decision.' He grinned, as Sam playfully hit him in the chest.

'Ouch!'

'Serves you right, she said as she ran ahead of him. Dave soon caught up as she said, "You know what I would like".

"A piggyback?" asked Dave.

"You'll never manage that now", she laughed. No, I'd like a steaming hot chocolate.'

'That can be arranged' he said, as they walked hand in hand back to the car, still admiring the bright sparkling lights, until it faded from their view. On the way home they bought four cups of hot chocolate.

They smiled as they found Alfie and Carol sound asleep together on the couch. Alfie was hanging halfway off but seemed comfortable enough. Sam went over and gently shook them. Carol opened her eyes and moved, as Dave came forward and picked Alfie up and carried him to his bedroom.

Carol apologised for not getting Alfie upstairs, but they both said it didn't matter as the three sipped their hot chocolate.

Dave finally said, 'You girls stay and chat if you want to, 'I'm going up.' No rush in the morning, great!'

Sam told Carol about them having a good heart to heart.

'You are a smashing family', Carol said, that is why you shouldn't have me around too much.

'Nonsense!' said Sam. Let's get you settled in your room'. Sam showed Carol where she'd left toiletries and towels for visitors. They sat on the bed and talked for a short while. Within those moments Tanya appeared to them with her bright red lipstick and dark hair. Holding onto each other they read Tanya's lips saying thank you, then she was gone again, as happily saying good night Sam gently shut the bedroom door behind her. Do I tell Dave about that? She questioned herself. It didn't matter either way, she decided. They are once again as close as ever and that's all that she needed.

It was decided that Carol would leave after breakfast. Dave was downstairs early studying the instructions on his drone.

'Dad's new toy', teased Alfie.

'Why not he said?' He looked up. Hope you girls bought something nice yesterday.'

'Thanks Dave, I bought some lovely leather gloves.

'Mine is a surprise, I'll show you later', said Sam. I have money left. We'll have to go on another shopping spree.'

'Fair enough', Dave said, still studying his drone, we can go to the park later.' Sam looked at Carol. 'Men and their toys!'

'I can take my new football, said Alfie. Dave was fine flying his drone and loving it. He and Alfie made up a game where Alfie kicked the ball and the drone had to follow it. He then hid it amongst the trees and the drown had to fly high, finding its exact hidden spot. Eventually Sam began to get cold and so they returned home.

She suddenly realized that Alfie was sitting pencil in hand. She looked at him, 'are these new too?' 'Yes mum'.

'Did you choose them?'

'Yes', he said grinning. Dad didn't have a clue what to buy me.'

'I love you, my clever boy' she said. You are so sensible and grown up, who else would think of buying something they could learn from without being told to?' Alfie was sitting with a new learning to write book, following over the alphabet shapes with one of his new pencils. She left him happily carrying on.

Chapter 17

Sam slowly began disliking coffee and was drinking fresh orange juice when Dave, now normally unknown, was home for breakfast. He gulped down his coffee noting that hers was still laying there. He crunched on his toast quickly. 'Running late', he said, pecking her on the cheek and heading for the front door. Alfie had just missed him. He ran to the window and banged on the glass managing to draw Dave's attention just enough for them to wave goodbye before he drove off.

After the school run Sam returned to the dishes and saw her coffee still there. Her mind began to churn. 'Could I be pregnant?' she half said to herself. I went off coffee when I was expecting Alfie.' After clearing up she went straight out and brought a Pregnancy Test Kit and waited stressed out before using it, and then, a few more minutes for the result. She was still stressed out, but excited at the same time. Positive! She yelped. She was off thinking again, considering what Dave and Alfie may say, then deciding to book an appointment with her Doctor. As luck would have it there was a slot free, she was pleased, at least the result would be finalized today and even before Alfie was home from school. The result at the surgery reassured her that she was indeed pregnant. Her blood pressure was also checked.

'Slightly high,' said her GP. Try to get some extra rest, although there is nothing to be over concerned about.'

Sam tried to keep calm while collecting Alfie from school. She wanted to have a normal evening with him, although her mind was swirling with thoughts. He had brought home a new reading book, she listened to him read and praised him to the heights.

Sam couldn't wait for Dave to get home that night. He kissed her as he walked in and sat beside her on the couch.

'Hungry?' she asked, trying to keep her voice stable. She ate with Alfie these days as she never knew what time Dave would get home, he didn't mind. She laid his food on the kitchen table and went to get him a beer out of the fridge. Upon her return he was already tucking into his pie, beans and chips. She was on tender hooks, just wanting to get the news out, but she didn't want Dave to choke on his dinner either. He ate quickly, cleared his plate and cutlery away and headed back to the couch with his beer where Sam was now sitting. 'I feel much better now' he said. What's new?'

Sam went for it. 'A baby!' she said. Dave turned his head sideways fast, now looking directly at her. 'A ... new... baby'... she said slowly.

'You're pregnant?'

'Yes!' said Sam simply. He picked her up and twirled her around.

'Sorry!' He put her down again. Are you sure, are you ok?' Dave was very excited.

'Calm down, you'll wake Alfie.' Then we can tell him, too'. He sat down. 'Wow!' 'I'm so happy!'

'I can tell', she laughed. They talked and laughed together, filled with joy.

Can we tell Alfie together?'

'Of course,'.

'I'll try and get home early, at least one night this week, if not we'll tell him together at the weekend. He grinned like a Cheshire cat!

Dave phoned Sam the following afternoon. 'Don't cook', he said I'll bring some burgers and stuff home for all of us. I'll be home nice and early to see Alfie'. Sam and Alfie were practicing Alfie's reading when they heard the key in the door. Alfie looked up in surprise. 'Dad?' Dave walked in and there were big hugs all around.

'Careful', said Dave moving gently away from his family in order to place the hot food on the table. They all tucked in enjoying the food. They knew that Alfie was of importance tonight, so leaving the dishes they guided Alfie to the couch and sat him between them. Dave began. 'We have a surprise for you son. Mum is going to have a baby. You will have a brother or sister.' Alfie just sat there.

'Isn't that wonderful?' asked Sam. Alfie shrugged his shoulders.

'Do you know what we mean?' asked Dave.

'Yes', said Alfie as he up and left.

'Perhaps he's shocked and confused,' said Sam. We'll mention it again when we put him to bed.'

Dave asked Alfie to finish reading his book with him,

hoping that Alfie would open up and talk to him. No chance! He just sat and read to Dave as he'd been asked to. He did need help with a few words but on the whole he got on great, after which he turned the television on. Not a word about the baby was mentioned by Alfie and when they tried to talk to him again at bedtime, he simply said 'I know mum is having a baby.'

Their excitement of telling him the good news was dampened by his behaviour. They left Alfie tucked in bed having told him that he could talk to them about the new baby whenever he wanted to. There was no response.

After the school run Sam rung Carol and was met with talking nonstop. 'Gosh! I was just going to phone you' she said. I have an appointment with Detective Campbell. Do you want to come along?

'What time?' 1.00 pm'.

'OK', said Sam. Neither knew if the news was going to be good or bad regarding Tanya.

They were led into Detective Campbell's office and he offered them a seat as he began. 'It has taken us a while to draw the pieces together and to find and apprehend the killer, but we now have him in custody. It seems that he obtained drugs to impress his friends and so the parties at your sister's flat were highly charged. After your neighbour gave us his description and other most valued information, his so-called friends began to contact us, informing us that he had stayed/hid with them and threatened their family's with violence should anyone report him. They had to keep quiet for their family's protection and safety. It was only after they heard that he had fled to Europe that they were willing to come forward. We are still talking to them. We probably will not impose any drug charges upon them.

Jack Turner was on his way back from Europe when he was apprehended. He was driving a stolen company vehicle and tried to say that he was a working driver, but we knew that the truck had been reported as stolen. He was dismissed from that company for dangerous driving that too, was probably drug related. We found these on him, Mrs. Glover Smith; do you know anything about them?'

Carol had a good look. 'I couldn't swear to it, but it certainly looks like the keys to Tanya's front door.'

'That's what we figured. It seems that he thought he was on safe ground and now he even had an empty flat at his disposal. Did your sister not mention a man at all?'

'No, she didn't'.

A tear fell from Carol's eye. She has held up so well thought Sam, as they sat mute.

'Are you alright hen?'

'Can we go home now? And soon they were sitting in the carpark still trying to get over the shock of all that they had just been told. Sam was the first to speak. 'Queenie could have been in much danger, but probably thought that she was safe.'

We need to see and talk to her', said Carol.

Time seemed to run away with them as they phoned her to see when they could visit. 'Oh! My dear' she said, hearing Carol's voice, the police have just phoned me.'

'Yes', said Carol. Sam and I have just returned from the police station. Are you alright?'

'Of course, dear'.

'I'm so sorry,' said Carol. You have been so wonderful and brave. Did they tell you that he was possibly on his way back to Tanya's? Tanya's, she emphasised, when they caught up with him. You have been in great danger. He would have probably realized it was you who informed the police regarding his wear-abouts. He might have even attacked you for his own means.'

'I am fine dear, don't you worry about me, but I would like to see you and Sam.' Carol looked at Sam.

'Next week, ok?' Sam gave her the thumbs up sign.

'I'm always here dears, come whenever you like.'

'We will ring you to arrange a time. Thank you so much Queenie for everything.' Carol clicked off her mobile.

Sam had to collect Alfie from school but before she left, she told Carol that visiting Queenie's on Thursday morning would be best for her. She'd remembered that her first Circle meeting was on Wednesday morning, giving her a chance to discuss any concerned issues experienced with Carol.

Chapter 18

Sam was excited but also nervous about going to her first circle meeting and wondered why they called it a circle. Today was the day she was going to find out. Jade was greeting those joining at the door telling them to take a seat, chairs were laid out in the form of a circle. One questioned answered, thought Sam. Once everyone had settled, Jade began to explain. 'We sit in a circle as this represents the circle of life. A never-ending circle. We believe that our present life does not stop once

we die our earthly death; our soul life continues on to the next life and often we have many lives.'

Sam listened intently. 'We are here to listen, learn and understand, not only from me, but from each other, this is very much a shared experience. We will learn by various methods including meditation and visualization, so let's get started.

We always open with a prayer, so can you shut your eyes and make sure your feet are planted firmly on the floor'. She said a prayer about welcoming each of them to the circle and hoped that those of the other worlds would join them, in time.

'Visualize your feet growing into the ground and taking

root, this way we are truly grounded'.' The next step was what Jade called opening up. For this we had to breathe gently and see (visualize) a golden thread at the top of our heads leading into the heavens. Jade explained the reason for this was to connect with those above but to also keep centred in this world. 'This is particularly difficult at the beginning of learning she said. A lot comes to us with practice and becomes quite natural in the end, rather like driving a car or riding a bicycle, the basic always returns, but for now let's carry on. So, to centre yourself, see before you a circle surrounding your feet. In the middle of this circle is a dot, if you ever drift away, bring your mind back to that dot and you will feel centred again, this will also make you feel protected. That is also why we also start and end with a prayer.'

Jade then conducted a meditation. She told of a garden; we are walking along its path. When we get to a gate someone is there to let us in. The group is to firstly visualize the hands of that person. Are they large or small male or female? Look at the person opening the gate from bottom to top. What is the person wearing on his/her feet? How is he/she dressed? What does the persons face look like? All of these aspects help with the learning and improving of our intuitive and psychic skills. Other exercises may hold the aspect of sensing smell, flowers for example. She said. 'When I ask you to return to the now, I will lead you back gently and each of you are to bring back what you have seen, heard and felt from this meditate experience, and to tell each other about it. What this teaches us most of all is to be in the moment. To switch off to our outer self and concentrate on thoughts and feelings of our inner being. In time we will connect with those from beyond this realm. Our Angels, Spirit Guides, relative and friends who have passed over (died) and all others who want to help us understand about our Spirituality and so will guide us on our amazing Spiritual journeys.' Sam really enjoyed her circle time, she learnt much and felt relaxed and at ease, just as Jade had said they would feel. They would continue to learn to totally tune into their meditative state, and they could use it as a tool to relax and refresh their daily lives.

Sam got a chance to tell Carol of her circle experience as they drove to Queenie's. Surprisingly, Carol did not say much, other then. 'I really need to talk to you about my psychic beginning; perhaps we could do that next week?'

'That will be good, said Sam. I have something very special to share with you as well.'

They smiled at each other. 'We spend quite a bit of time together, but it never seems enough.'

'You are right' said Sam' as Carol pulled into a parking space in the grounds of Queenie's flat. Queenie was thrilled to see them. The tea tray was once again out with biscuits on a side plate. Soon after greeting each other there was much chatter over tea, Carol once again thanking Queenie for her help in finding Tanya's boyfriend killer. Carol couldn't bear to use his name, although she remembered it. Once again, she also told Queenie how brave she'd been. Queenie merely smiled, waving her hand as if to say it was nothing at all as Carol said. 'I have the key to Tanya's flat, would both of you like to come next door with me?'

They nodded in unison and when they had finished eating and drinking, they went next door.

The flat was tidy and neat with basic furniture and older kitchen fittings. All the rooms were bright and light looking. The bedroom had a double bed and usual furniture, again everything being neat, clean and tidy, even the sprinkles of dust seemed to fit into the flat, like an extra layer of light, rather than dust. Sam could see that Carol was getting upset as Queenie asked. 'What will you do with this place, dear? It is so sweet in its own way.'

'I don't know. I still need to work out all these issues.

'You could live next door to me, dear', said Queenie. Carol shrugged her shoulders, as a tear spilled out of her eye and others were beginning to join in. They both went to Carol and gave her a hug. Sam headed for the front door and as she did, she saw a flash of Tanya. This time she managed to read her bright red lips, 'thank you', were her words. They went back to Queenie's and chatted and had more tea, leaving her place much later than they had intended.

Sam could see that Carol was in deep thought on the drive back.

'I saw Tanya just then', Sam told Carol.

'I sensed her', replied Carol. Sam did not say anything, instead, she touched Carol's arm in a warm gesture as Carol drove home blinking back the tears. They arranged to meet at the end of the following week.

Chapter 19

Alfie was home from school playing with his Lego once again. Sam asked. 'How was school?

'OK'.

'Just, OK? Wash your hands please love.'

Alfie disappeared and returned within a few minutes. They began eating is silence when Alfie suddenly asked, 'When will the baby come, mum?'

'A few months yet, smiled Sam, are you looking forward to it?'

'No! Snapped Alfie shoving his fork into his mouth. I don't even want it!' He gulped down some of his drink and left the table without asking to be excused. Sam was startled and annoyed leaving her own food she went to him. He was already back playing with his toys, his face like thunder. She took the toy out of his hand.

'You do not behave like that young man. Talk to me and I will help, I always will, I love you too much to do any less, but I will not put up with downright bad behaviour.'

Alfie burst into tears. Sam went over and cuddled him. 'Talk to me love, what is the matter? I can't help you if you won't tell me what is troubling you. Why don't you want a little brother or sister? 'Mummy', he said. Sam noticed the mummy, rather than mum. Will you and daddy still love me?' Sam noticed the daddy, as well. He was reverting into being a small child again.

'Oh! Alfie. Dad and I will not only love you, but I will also need your help. You and your baby sister or brother will be wonderful friends, I am sure. You are too nice a little boy not to just like but love your new sibling. Do you know what sibling means?

'Baby' said Alfie.

'Nearly' smiled Sam. It means brother or sister', that way you don't have to say him or her, or even it when we talk about the baby what?

'Sibling', giggled Alfie.

'That's the giggle I love'. She kissed the top of his head and rubbed his back as he stood next to her. 'How can I help you with the baby?' he grinned when my sibling comes.'

'You could cuddle the baby. Maybe get me some nappies or bottles when I need them. Lots of little bits and pieces, but important things'.

'I will be at school, though, and dad will be at work.'

'True, said Sam, but there will be plenty of weekends and your school holidays when you can help me.'

Slowly, but surely, Alfie became his old self during the evening. Surprisingly, Dave was home earlier than of late. He went straight upstairs to say good night to Alfie. Sam could hear Alfie talking about how he was going to help with the baby, and that he was going to be a proper big brother.

'That is just what the baby will be looking for', said Dave. A proper big brother.'

'What was that all about?' Dave asked getting to the bottom of the stairs.

Sam told him the whole story while he ate his meal. 'You're home earlier, that's nice' she said.

'For me too', he replied, giving her a kiss and touching her growing tummy.

Sam and Carol met for lunch and a catch up as planned. Remembering her conversation with Sam sitting in her first circle, Carol said that she would like to tell Sam something of her childhood and the psychic area of her life.

'Please do, said Sam. I've wanted to know more about you for a very long time.'

Carol began by saying that from a very early age she felt different from other children. 'More caring and sensitive I suppose, but I didn't understand my feelings, I just felt odd and out of place. I knew things, like the telephone was going to ring and who was going to be on the other end. A lot of young children get these feelings, mostly at the toddler stage, as they haven't been too far outside the home environment yet. For me it started at that age, but it became a regular occurrence even in later life. I would tell my mum things in excitement, very pleased when I was right, but my mum would say to me, 'that was a good guess'.

'There were many incidents, strange experiences I went through which I wished mum would have talked to me about, especially as I grew older, but she never did. She just seemed to close herself down and me with her. Growing up Tanya and myself were great together, just us and mum. I can't even remember a time when dad was around, but mum never spoke of that either. If we asked, all she said was that he left; we don't need to know the ins and outs, as she put it, and we accepted that. Perhaps all children just listened and accepted in those days. Tanya and I did not talk about our so-called psychic experiences, we did not know that we had abilities; we thought that all our experiences were just games. I remembered a game which we played called imaginary friends and we often had the same friends in this game. We would describe the person, their looks, and their dress and so on and tell the other. 'I see her/him there.' Only then would we realize that we were pointing at the same place. We really thought that this was a game which only the two of us ever played, that's how our lives were as children. When we grew up, we never spoke about anything on those lines, even though, at times, we were really close. Now, I wonder if our abilities only came to us at a certain time and for a certain reason, such as Tanya needing your help in order to find and reconnect with me, so as to help her find peace again. I never thought of any of this for years, not even when I was with John. Things began to come back to me after meeting you.' The friends spoke of all of this, as they sat at their tiny table in the corner of the restaurant. Carol continued.

'It was only just before mum died, from cancer, that she told me that what I experience comes down the line from her mother, my grandmother. She said that she was afraid of that side of life, was how she put it, and so tried to get rid of it for me. She told me not to follow that route, but that if I felt the need to, then to be careful with it. I did follow it for a while, but the interest seemed to come and go with me.

John never knew anything about it. He never appeared to me after he died, making me loose interest even more. Although the people at the Spiritualist Church know me it's been more recently that I started going again and not on any regular basis.'

'My turn' said Sam with a big smile.

'What? You look like the cat that had all the cream.' Sam's smile got bigger and wider until she beamed. 'I'm pregnant' she said. Carol got up, making a loud noise while dragging her chair away from the table. She hugged Sam.

'Congratulations! What did the family have to say?'

'Oh!' said Carol, pretending to sound very dramatic.

'What? Said Carol again, this time sounding unsure of the response she might get.

'It's ok' laughed Sam. Dave is over the moon. Alfie has been a bit up and down with the news, but he's all for it now. Says he wants to be a proper big brother. The beam on Sam's face never faded.

'I can see how happy you are', Carol smiled.

'That's until the labour and the sleepless nights begin. Only kidding' Sam laughed.

'How far along are you?'

'Nearly three months, my first scan is due soon.' Sam continued to smile, but wondered if there were regrets in Carol's life, and took the bull by the horns. 'Did you and John not want children?' she asked. She bit her lip and wished she hadn't approached the subject when she saw the sad look in Carol's eyes.

'It simply didn't happen'.

'I'm sorry, said Sam, reaching across the table and touching her hand. Carol shrugged in response.

'I guess it wasn't meant to be'.

They sat quietly for a while. 'Anyway' Sam said. You can be part of my family, all my family, we need to go out and celebrate and you must come too.'

'That would be lovely, see what your family have to say.' Carol still sounded sad, so Sam left things as they were as they hugged goodbye before getting into their separate cars.

At the dinner table Sam talked about meeting Carol for lunch, telling Dave and Alfie how pleased she was for all of them with the baby due.

'I told her you want to be a proper big brother' she said to Alfie.

'I do' he said, putting on his best proud face.

After putting Alfie to bed Dave and Sam sat together, just relaxing. Dave laid his hand on Sam's tummy saying, 'I love you all and I love this baby already, was I like this will Alfie?'

'You tried to be, but I was working, really tired when I came home and all I wanted was early nights. Other times I would fall asleep on the couch, then suddenly wake up with your hand on my tummy, just like now, and you would be chatting away to the baby. Sometimes, pretending to sleep, I would

watch and listen to you talking some more. Five years ago, I can't believe that Sam said. Oh! by the way, I told Carol that we want to go out and celebrate the baby coming and that she can come along too. Dave looked shocked 'When? Where? Why?' Don't you want to?' asked Sam.

'Of-course', said Dave. You just take my breath away sometimes, with your surprise thoughts and deeds.'

'We'll sort something out and I need to tell Queenie, also.'

'Queenie, Carol's, sister's neighbour?'

'Yes'. We are all friends now of-course I want to tell her.' '

OK', laughed Dave. I'm happy if you want to tell all these people.'

'Who have you told?' Sam asked.

'Nobody'. '

What?' '

Well, I'll tell the lads from the pub, but the others are just work colleges. Sighing, Sam said.

'Men are strange'.

Chapter 20

Sam's routine was much the same the following morning and upon her return from the school run she felt slightly tired. She decided to sit and read and so she read through her local newspaper. It reminded her of how her and Carol met through Tanya, her spirit now being that of a murder victim. She dwelled on the strange events which sometimes overtook her complete life. Suddenly she felt an odd sensation inside her. She cupped her hands around her baby bump saying. 'Welcome baby. We love you.' A peaceful awareness overcame her. She didn't want to come away from this gentle world, but she had to and far too quickly, as she heard a strange dull banging sound. Listening hard she realized that it was someone banging on her front door, where she found a little girl standing on her doorstep crying. Before she could make much sense of anything the police and an ambulance were arriving.

She picked up the toddler and cuddled her, turning her face away from what was taking place across the street, as she watched a man been taken away in handcuffs and a policewoman appeared on her pathway, asking if they could go indoors. Sam was still carrying the crying child in her arms. The policewoman went into Sam's kitchen and got a glass of water offering it to the toddler now seated on Sam's lap. The child took a few sips between her sobs. There was a noisy bang on the door which the policewoman answered. A lady walked into Sam's house, as the toddler immediately got off Sam's lap and ran to her. 'Thank you, thank you' she said to Sam. I am Zoe's Aunt.'

The policewoman walked out of Sam's house with them, as Sam stood at her window watching them drive away. Sam was totally in shock. The policewoman returned.

'A colleague of mine will be in to talk to you soon' she said to Sam. Almost on queue there was a knock on the door again and in walked Detective Thomas Campbell.

'You can go now. I'll take things from here' he said to the policewoman, who immediately left.

'Hello! Again Mrs. James', Detective Campbell's voice sounded surprised.

'Detective Campbell. What is going on? Sam asked.

'It seems Mrs. James that you are involved in yet another murder case.

'What? I was just sitting here minding my own business.'

'I know, hen' he began. Sorry, Mrs. James, I should say.'

Sam was getting irritated. What on earth has happened? She looked out of the window saying, 'the place is surrounded by police, the press are out there and an ambulance was here earlier. I even saw a man being taking away in handcuffs. I need to know what's happening.'

'Yes, you do. I will start at the beginning. We received a 999 call from a neighbour saying she could hear a child crying hysterically and that it had been going on for a while.

We had a car on the way over when a second call came in from the same person saying that the child was still crying and now also screaming, alongside the scream of a woman as well.

'Did you know them, the neighbours across the road?'

'No. I had no idea who lived there, never saw anyone around.'

'The man taken away, continued Detective Campbell was the lady's husband, sadly, he had stabbed her. He has admitted to it already, saying it was in a fit of temper after a huge argument. It will be all over the news soon, anyway. Can you come into the station and give us a statement? Tell us how the little girl came to be with you and what you saw taking place. How old would you say the child was?'

'Around three to four years old. I would say nearer three, but she must be a very clever little girl to have come and knocked on my door'.

'Yes', we still have many areas of this crime to cover but thank you. When would you like to go to the station?'

'How about now', said Sam, before I get my son from school.'

'Would you like a lift there and back? You look shocked and overwhelmed.'

'That would be most helpful'.

Detective Campbell spoke to one of the policemen outside and it was sorted. Sam grabbed her handbag and they were off. Detective Campbell headed for his own car. Sam figured he was going somewhere else and not back to the police station.

Samantha

Sam was glad that everyone had left the street by the time she had returned home from the police station as she didn't want Alfie confronted with all that had been going on. She let herself in, still wondering why suddenly trouble seemed to come her way. She wondered about Dave and felt sure that he would definitely want them to move away now. She suddenly felt exhausted, setting her mobile alarm, just in case, she told herself, she only woke up when it rang. Splashing some cold water on her face to freshen up, she headed for Alfie's school.

Returning, she still felt unsettled, but did not get too much time to dwell on the situation as Alfie kept chattering about school. She listened and responded to him and later they went over his reading book together, feeling very pleased that he had returned to his old self again, thanks to Dave's reassurance that he would still be very much loved, even after the baby arrives. He had now got into the habit of saying, 'Night! Night!' while touching Sam's tummy before turning over onto his side to fall asleep. Sam thought this was really cute, and encouraged his involvement, sometimes he even kissed Sam's tummy, as if he were kissing the baby.

Dave was happy as it was his night out with his friends and he was looking forward to telling them about the baby. Sam didn't want to spoil his good mood, but she felt it necessary to tell him about what had happened earlier.

'There is something you need to know, love, she began. Dave gave her a 'not again' look and he was right. There was an incident in the house across the road. The toddler came and banged on the door crying. I looked after her, there were police and confusion everywhere. Amongst it all Detective Campbell turned up so I've already given a statement.'

'God!' said Dave. Are you all safe? Do you want me to stay home tonight?'

'No love, no', said Sam. You just needed to know'.

'What happened for the child to come here' asked Dave, he needed to know everything in order to protect his family.

'It seems began Sam, taking a deep breath, that the couple had an almighty fight, the toddler ran over here. I saw the police take the man away in handcuffs, and Detective Campbell tells me that he in custody having admitted to stabbing her.'

'I'm not going out', said Dave. You shouldn't be put under all this stress.'

I'm fine, love. You go out. I need an early night anyway.' In the end Dave cleared and tidied up the kitchen while Sam relaxed. He realized that Sam possibly needs extra help and care as she carries this baby and looks after Alfie and himself. He did go out and had a good night, celebrating the news of the baby with his friends, but he did return home early and his friends understood perfectly. He found Sam tucked up in bed. He checked on Alfie, he found him quietly snoring in his bed; all was well with his little family. He got himself ready and lay beside Sam placing his arm over her tummy. She did not stir, but he did feel the baby move. With a feeling of pride and contentment, he relaxed and fell into a sound, peaceful, sleep.

Alfie came down to breakfast surprised to see Dave.

'Dad!'

'Hi Son.' 'What are you doing at home?'

'Only for a short time. Mum and I have to go somewhere special and then I will go back to work.'

Alfie looked at Sam pouring milk onto his cereal. He looked at Dave, then back at Sam saying. 'To see the baby?' They looked at each other in surprise as Alfie continued tucking into his breakfast.

'What do you mean Alfie?' asked Sam.

'I know that it is a girl mum' he said, as cool as a cucumber. His parents looked at each other, shocked again, but Alfie did not even flinch. Dave drove Alfie to school, which pleased him no end. Driving to the hospital Dave said. 'Do you think it is a girl?'

'Maybe, or maybe Alfie just guessed' replied Sam, sensing that Dave was getting confused and railed up because of Alfie's perceptive words. It's too early to tell. Anyway, and do we want to know which it is? Or do we want a nice surprise?' She tried to sound quirky and funny, but it seemed that Dave was in no mood for fun.

'I think we already know. Alfie has somehow managed to tell us where we are going, and what sex the baby is' said Dave, sounding annoyed.

'I don't know what to say, so why don't we just enjoy these special moments and forget about Alfie's words.' To Sam's delight, Dave managed a smile as he pulled into the hospital carpark.

Sam and Dave did not have to wait too long before they were called in for their baby's scan. The radiographer knew from Sam's records that they would know the procedure so went ahead with getting Sam onto the bed and the equipment set up. Sam tightened at the feel of the cold gel, but soon settled again as Dave stood next to her holding her hand. The radiographer had a good look at the screen first, and then turned it around for Dave and Sam. They both felt very excited at seeing the baby's tiny, fast beating heart, as the nurse explained that its measurements were perfect for the growing baby and passed onto them the baby's due date.' The thrill of seeing this tiny form moving around took their breath away, and everything else completely dissolved out of their minds. They felt an immense amount of love for the baby as they held hands tightly and took those beautiful moments into their hearts to keep locked away for ever. A copy of their baby's scan was before them, now to be taken home and kept alongside Alfie's. They left the hospital on cloud nine! Dave had a quick cup of tea with Sam before returning to work.

Sam collected Alfie from school. He was his usual happy go lucky self, chatting away on the ride home. Sam was disappointed that the topic of the baby didn't come up, but she felt that it was best to leave things as they were. It was much later when Alfie kissed the baby Night! Night! That he looked at Sam's tummy in a different way. He then looked at her and said, 'Grace saw you and Dad this morning, she says she loves us all. Sam was taken aback, but jumped in quickly with, 'How do you know these things, love?'

'I don't know how, but words just come into my head.'

'Does it frighten you?'

'No, but Dad doesn't like it, does he?'

'It's because he doesn't understand what is happening to you, this makes him feel like that he can't look after or protect you, so he worries.

'And you both fight about it.' Alfie looked sad.

'I wish he was here now to hear you talk about this. You sound so grown up and seem to accept everything that you hear, where-as we don't accept, so we are always questioning things. I am getting slightly better, but Dad still struggles. Do you know what I mean, Alfie?' He nodded in reply and smiled at Sam.

'I heard everything', said Dave as Sam turned around in surprise.

'I've been listening and watching both of you. He walked towards them. Alfie sat up and all three hugged. As they pulled apart Dave said.

'I'll try harder to accept, but it is not easy. Sam lay Alfie down gently as Dave ruffled his hair and gave him a good night kiss. He smiled happily as they left his bedroom.

They sat together in the kitchen, Sam drinking tea as Dave ate his meal. They were still both stunned at Alfie. 'What do you make of your five-year-old son who knows things he shouldn't? Who hears things no one else can hear and is happy to tell us all about it?' They could find no words to explain Alfie's awareness, let alone trying to find the right ones.

When Dave had finished eating, he went into the living room. Sam tided up, loaded the dish washer and joined him, taking with her a glass of juice and a beer. Dave took her hand.

'Just look after yourself and Alfie that's all I ask. If you feel uncomfortable about anyone or any situation, please, just pull away from it. Get yourself and Alfie as far away as quickly as possible.

'You said it yourself Sam I don't know how to help or protect you and Alfie.' They smiled at each other, both glad that they were slowly coming to terms with Alfie's ways and Sam's learning process. They hoped that this togetherness would last, but that was left to be seen, taking one more opportunity of this good evening together she asked. 'What do you think of the name Grace?' Dave looked at her puzzled. She took a deep breath while trying to speak with humour in her voice laughing gently.

'Well!' she said. According to our son, who knows all, our daughter, he says, likes the name Grace and that's what she wants to be named. Grace. Alfie already calls her that.

Dave threw his arms up in the air. 'I give up, he laughed. Is Alfie ruling the roost, or what? Sam shrugged as they giggled together. 'As it happens, I like that name, how about you?'

'I feel as if I know her by that name already' answered Sam.

'Then Grace it is' they said in unison as Sam quickly grabbed Dave's hand and laid it on her tummy. They felt the movement of the baby; it felt as if she was jumping for joy! 'Our baby Grace', said Dave, bending down and kissing Sam's tummy. Sam laughed. 'I'm sure Grace must hold the record for being the most kissed baby, yet to be born'.

Sam was now anxious to tell Queenie about the baby as her and Carol agreed upon a day to visit. Carol mentioned to Sam that she felt it was time to start the business of sorting out Tanya's flat.

They had tea with Queenie. It was laid out in its usual fashion, including the teacups and saucers. They talked and laughed together. Queenie was excited about Sam's baby and Sam promised that she would get to meet her whole family sometime. They both noticed that Carol seemed slightly on edge. Queenie eventually asked. 'What is it dear? You don't seem right today.'

'I've also come here to sort out Tanya's flat, not a nice job, would both of you come with me?' They all headed out with a trembling hand Carol unlocked the front door. They were taken aback with the stench of stale food, drink and who knows what else! They opened windows and left the front door open to let in some fresh air.

'Sorry, I should have come in alone.'

'Not at all dear,' said Queenie. After the initial shock, Queenie suggested that she pop next door and get some bleach. Having checked Tanya's cupboards first they found mops and other cleaning materials, soon, the big clean up began. Between the three, the flat was soon looking cleaner, fresher and smelt really good. Carol checked for paperwork in all the drawers, there was far more around than she expected so she decided to take it all to her house and look at it, hopefully in a calmer, more organized manner than she felt at the time. She told Queenie and Carol that she would sort out Tanya's clothes and other items at a later date.

'At least the flat is mine' she said. I don't have to worry

about people coming to look at it, at least not for the moment.'

Chapter 21

Sitting quietly in her big house Carol looked around wondering if she should move into Tanya's flat, just a small two bedroomed place, cosy and comfy. No garden to worry about, less cleaning, not so much chance of collecting too much unnecessary stuff, she allowed her mind to drift. Unfortunately, it drifted to her couch where her beloved husband had died, looking at the couch she felt sad, lost and un-loved. She did a double take as she saw a flash of John 'Stupid! She scolded herself; it's all in my head! As if in response she felt a hand on her shoulder, lightly, but with enough weight for it to be real, and heard the words 'I love you'. Carol began to cry; she sobbed and sobbed until there were no more tears left to shed. Suddenly, her feelings of being un-loved disappeared. It was replaced by warmth, a glowing of heat all around her body she lifted up her head, saying to the air. 'You have come to say goodbye, darling. You are right; it is time for me to move on. I will figure it all out and carry on with my life John.'

The cushion on the couch fell to the floor, the lights flickered. John was definitely around. Sensing him in the air their souls connected, now she was un-afraid. 'We each have our own paths to follow, our own journeys to make, but we will meet again, my love, you and I', she said in her head. Carol was still sad, but forging forward was her aim, for it was the right time, she felt it in her body and soul.

Feeling at peace about John and her circumstances led her to start checking Tanya's paperwork. She settled at her desk with a cup of tea as many envelopes lay before her, far more than she could have ever imagined. Two columns were arranged, one for bills the other for general mail. She began checking the bills, everything was in good order thanks to her transferring Tanya's bills into her bank account and checking her statement each month to make sure that they were being paid. Sadness began creeping in again, for the two people who meant the most to her were now gone, but alongside this was a feeling of accomplishment as slowly, but surely, her path was moving in the right direction. The second pile was harder, opening the topmost one first she checked who it was signed by, Jacky, it said. The letter asked if Tanya was ok. It questioned why she was rushing away after the workday, and why she did not socialise with any of her work colleagues anymore. Carol opened about four more; they were pretty much on the same lines. Sighing she said aloud, 'Tanya darling, if only you could have confided in someone, your work mates seemed to know that something was wrong.' This tone of letters continued. One even asked. Are you still with your boyfriend? Her mind adrift with thoughts Carol felt that Tanya and her colleagues must have been close once. Why else would Tanya have spoken about him? In another letter she noticed that her boyfriend was even mentioned by name, Jack. Where are these friends now, she wondered, there didn't seem many people at her funeral. She wondered if she should trace them, but then remembered that at the end she didn't even know which company Tanya was working for.

Carol's mind went into overdrive. Gone was her time of peace and strength. Back was the time of sadness for Tanya and for the terrible lifestyle she must have been forced to lead toward the end. Carol took a break from the letters and sat quietly sipping her freshly made tea, allowing the warmth to enter her body, but it did not warm her up, she was cold and sad once again.

Carol began to realize that Queenie's observations were spot on. How at first Tanya and Jack were an ordinary couple walking in the gardens happily. Later, she seemed very alone and unsettled not wondering too far away from the flat to be seen. Forcing someone to physically appear and sometimes even man handle her back indoors. Now, these letters were telling of how she rushed away after work, meaning that she wasn't allowed to socialize with her friends anymore. All of these incidents fitted in with the police account of the tragic circumstances which led to Tanya's sudden death.

Tears were spilling again, but with-it Carol's strength began to return. She began drying up her tears and with that notion vowed to continue with her life. She looked at the next envelope and was stunned to see John's name on it, a letter he never received perhaps? Or a letter he read, and left with Tanya, for safe keeping, so as Carol would not see it? Or maybe see it at a later date, just as she was seeing it now? In it Tanya thanked John for looking after her. For finding her a safe place, a hotel room in which to stay, making it a place where she could literary run to once Jack was too drunk or stoned to notice her gone. She wrote of how the peace and tranquillity she gained in a good, peaceful, night's sleep kept her functioning through his demanding, bullying behaviour. Tanya's letter said that she was sorry, for she sensed that Carol thought that something was going on between them. It's ironic, she wrote, we both stayed in the same hotel, you watched out for me, but the one thing that Carol was afraid of didn't even occur to us. We didn't want to hurt her, yet we managed to do just that! Carol's large tear drops flooded the note paper. She mopped them up with a tissue and read on. Oh! How I regret not sharing an explanation of our behaviour with Carol, Tanya continued, but you and I know that it was for her own safety. We were both afraid that if I stayed at your house that Jack may find me and that would place Carol in danger, for he wanted that power. Another woman under his thumb would be right up his street! I know I made your life horrible John. I knew you felt torn between Carol and me. I should have taken your first suggestion and moved right away from this area I am so sorry! I never intended to come between you and Carol in any way. I'm so glad that I persuaded you to go home in the end. You and Carol belong together and I had to make that right for all of us. I'm truly sorry for bringing my troubles to your door. Be happy again with Carol; be happy for all of us. Carol began to sob and she sobbed, until she felt a cold chill around her. Her cheek indented with the pressure of a kiss. She heard a voice, 'I'm sorry, I love you', it said, as out of the corner of her eye she saw Tanya standing as a solid figure as her bright red lips formed the words.

'Forgive me'. Carol smiled. Quick as a flash Tanya was gone.

'Goodbye, my lovely sister' Carol said aloud and with that, calmness overcame her, alongside feelings of happiness, sadness and exhaustion. There was one last letter to open. It was addressed to her. She did not feel the need to read it there and then, tomorrow will do she thought and went to bed.

While Carole was going through so many mixed emotions, Sam's life began to take on a slower pace. Perhaps it was nature making her slow down, allowing her to enjoy her pregnancy, to find time just to sit, hands around her tummy and think about her baby. She still thought of the baby as her daughter Grace and wondered if it would make a difference if it turned out to be a boy. She thought about how good she felt after her circle meetings and how by practicing her meditations she now found herself meeting the spirit of loved ones, her guides and others. The logic of it did not matter, in fact there seemed no logic involved, that was the point, it was over and above what our everyday lives offer us. What she experienced came from within! Sam enjoyed her time in circle, it brought her peace, it taught her many unknown skills and broadened her mind beyond recognition, all of which she loved.

Alfie was also keeping her busy; he'd made some new friends and asked Sam if they could come over after school.

Sam was all for it, she never did understand why he hadn't brought friends home or been invited to others houses previously as he was always surrounded by other children at school. His friends were there now, sitting around the table eating chicken nuggets, chips and peas, as they talked and laughed, but, at the same time Alfie kept watching each one of them in turn, strange behaviour, thought Sam. After pudding they headed to Alfie's bedroom. They could be heard having fun. Sam was relieved all seemed well as she began clearing up. Suddenly, she noticed and heard a child behind her. 'What's wrong?' she asked the crying child.

'Alfie told me that my Grandad says that I should join the school football team. I was trying to decide if I want to or not. Anyway, Alfie then said to me, 'Your Grandad is dead, isn't he?

I said, 'How do you know?' And he told me that my Grandad was standing behind me and how he was dressed. He's never seen my Grandad before so it upset me. Is he right, Mrs. James? Can he see my Grandad?

Sam bent down and said, 'don't cry love, I'll sort Alfie out.'

'Alfie!' she called.

'What?'

'Don't be so rude. Come down here, now!' Alfie thumped down the stairs. You've made your friend cry. That's not very nice.'

'He shouldn't be such a baby' retorted Alfie. He's lucky I saw his Grandad; he does want him to play football on the team.'

'See!' said the child, looking directly at Sam. With all the children now downstairs Sam had a quick glance at her watch. With a relieved smile she said, 'You are all tired. Your mums' will be here soon. Why don't all of you start getting your things together?' Alfie was about to follow them when Sam grabbed his arm firmly but gently. 'You stay near me' she said, giving Alfie one of her stares. Sam was lucky; by the time the boys had got their back packs and other bits together their mum's were on the doorstep. The upset child, Tom, was fine so Sam let things go, and waved him off home alongside the other children.

'What was that all about?' she asked Alfie sternly.

'You already know', he sulked.

'Then, we need to talk, sit down!' Alfie sat on the sofa swinging his legs. He had a worried look on his face. '

'Ok' Sam said. Maybe you do know things; so, the answer is that you have to learn from now when you say things to people and when you don't.' Alfie looked at her. Don't pretend you don't know what I am talking about!' Alfie's brave and rude attitude soon dissolved as he said. 'Help me mum!'

Sam went over to him as sitting beside him she placed a loving, protective arm around his shoulder. 'We shall help each other', she said smiling. Alfie managed a smile in return.

It was easy for Sam to speak of her and Alfie helping each other, but she had no real idea how this was going to happen. She was sitting mulling over this the following morning when her thoughts were interrupted by a phone call from the school. The school secretary phoned to say that the Head teacher wanted to see her after school if that was possible.

She agreed. Waiting on pins, wondering if this was in reference to the previous evening or something new as of today. She hoped that if it was to do with Tom that maybe the two mums could have sorted out the problem and it had not been taken it into the school.

Upon her arrival Alfie was handed over to her by his class teacher and he was told to go to Mr. Brown's office with his mum.

'What's going on Alfie?' she asked as they walked down the corridor.

'I got in a fight with Tom.' She was about to ask more when she saw Tom and his mother already sitting and waiting. The Head came out just as they arrived and ushered all four of them into his office.

'Mrs. James and Mrs. Harris, it seems Alfie and Tom were about to come to blows, fists raised at each other, luckily an adult managed to intervene. Neither will say what they were fighting about or why. 'Alfie!' he called, making him jump. What do you have to say?'

'Sorry Tom', said Alfie.

'Tom?' questioned Mr. Brown.

'Sorry Alfie'.

'Well, that's better' said Mr. Brown. How long have you been in this school, Tom?'

'Three days Mr. Brown'.

'And you Alfie?' Alfie had to think.

'A long time Mr. Brown.'

'You were supposed to look after Tom, Alfie, not fight with him'.

Mrs. Harris spoke up.

'Mr. Brown, they are five years old. I'm sure your school could have handled this, rather than calling us mum's in. She took a breath. 'Or else told us about it over the phone and we could have sorted it out ourselves.' Sam nodded in agreement.

'Well, Mrs. Harris, we like to nip these things in the bud and of course we like the parents to know first-hand what is happening. This is our school procedure', said the Head, sounding very pompous.

'Thank you', said Mrs. Harris as she stood up taking Tom by the hand. Sam followed suit and thanked Mr. Brown as they left his office. As they walked down the hallway both boys' left their mum's hand and walked together talking and laughing.

'I'm sorry,' said Sam. They had a bit of a disagreement at mine last night, did Tom tell you?'

'Yes, he did, it was something about Alfie seeing his Grandad, but I think he is still grieving for him. My dad passed away only a month ago.

'I'm so sorry', said Sam. I'll have a word with Alfie'.

To Sam's surprise Mrs. Harris asked. 'Would you like to meet for a coffee after we've dropped the boys' off in the morning, or do you have to rush to work?' Slightly taken aback Sam said, 'Yes that will be nice.' She then wondered if that was a good idea, or would it complicate their lives even more. So much for my peaceful days, she thought, and knew she had to tell Dave everything for she had promised that there would be no more secrets.

They were both quiet on the way home, until Alfie said. 'What will Dad say now?'

'I have no idea Alfie. We will all talk about it during or after dinner.

Dave knew that something was wrong as soon as he stepped through the door.

'Where's Alfie?'

'I sent him to his room and told him to get ready for bed. I'm glad you are home while he's still up.' 'Oh! Dear, Alfie in trouble?' Sam nodded as she placed Dave's food before him. '

'Knowing things?'

'Yes. I was going to tell you last night, but the evening ran away with us, then today the school rang and so another family has become involved.'

Dave seemed starved. Sam watched as he shovelled in his food.

'The two boys who came over last evening are new to the school. All this time he has nobody, and then two arrive. Anyway, Alfie apparently saw Tom's Grandad.'

Dave choked and coughed. 'Sorry', Sam said. Dave got up and got himself a glass of water. He sipped the water and stopped eating for a while. 'Alfie says that Tom wanted to know if he should join the school football team, so Alfie told him that he'd just seen and spoken to his Grandad and he says that Tom should. Of-course the poor boy freaked out when Alfie told him this. He came downstairs crying. I questioned Alfie, only for him to be very rude and cheeky to me, but he felt bad about frightening Tom. He can't help seeing and hearing things, but as I told him; he's going to have to learn how to use his knowledge, his knowing, in the correct way. At the moment things come to him, or he sees things and words come out of his mouth before he can think it through and stop them. I told him I would help him. The child was ok before he left, so I didn't say anything to his mum about it. I was sitting here trying to work out how to go about helping Alfie when I got the phone call to come into the school.

'Take it easy, babe. I'm trying to keep calm; one of us riled up is enough. I can see our baby growing and you need to rest and relax. If by just listening to you helps, then that is what I will do. I understand now that neither you nor Alfie can help the way you are, but you are right we have to help Alfie understand himself. He needs someone or something, like what do you call it, your circle? To help him.'

'I don't know how to help Alfie, but I'm going to look into it, ok? I'm sure there must be other children like him out there; I need to find out about that. I can talk to Carol, people in my circle and I will even check the Internet. I'm sure we can help him, but not on our own.'

'That's fine, babe. I'll talk to Alfie when I go upstairs, but Sam happened to go up first and found Alfie in bed crying. She was about to speak to him when Dave said, 'It's ok, babe, I'll handle this.' Sam left Alfie's room and went into their own. Dave lifted Alfie into a seated position and cuddled him. 'We'll help you son, he said, but you'll have to help yourself by listening to what you are being told. Alfie nodded. And no more being rude to your mum!' Alfie nodded again. Dave ruffled his hair.

'Are you on this football team?'

'No! I don't like football that much', he grinned.

'All ready for bed?'

'Yes, Dad'.

'Good! And remember your mum needs to relax and rest when she can.

'Grace is getting bigger, isn't she?

'Yes'.

'So, you look after your mum'. They hugged, and then Alfie lay down.

Dave popped his head into their bedroom only to find Sam sound asleep on top of the covers. By the time he had cleared the kitchen and sat down to a beer Sam was downstairs again.

'Hi! Sleeping Beauty, he said, want a drink or anything?'

'Bed please' was Sam's reply as she kissed him goodnight and headed back upstairs. He heard the sound of the shower and he felt happy and contended. In time he got himself sorted for bed and crawled in gently alongside Sam. He looked lovingly at his wife and soon to be mother again. He then placed his hand on her tummy and felt the strongest kick ever, the force of which woke Sam up with a start. 'It's ok' he whispered. Our baby is just showing how much she/he loves us.' Sam was just so tired; she sighed and promptly went back to sleep.

Dave never had dreams, or he didn't remember them, expect for the one he had that night. He related his dream to Sam the following morning. 'It was one about a little girl playing in a huge garden surrounded by many beautifully shaped and coloured flowers. Each flower was so vivid and real that I believed that they were not of this world, the colours and scents were so superior. I was almost convinced that I was in another land!'

'Not you, too,' laughed Sam. While those other worlds come here to visit Alfie and me, you go to other worlds to visit them.' Dave went pale as he rushed off to work.

Chapter 22

Sam was still tired, as absent-mindedly she felt her tummy. Alfie saw Sam as she arrived downstairs. He went over and kissed her tummy saying, 'Grace says good morning mummy.'

'You heard that, did you Alfie?' Sam's tone was rough, edgy, bordering on annoyance.

'There's your breakfast, eat it!' She pushed a bowl of cereal before him and turned away to get herself a cup of tea. Alfie ate his breakfast quietly, wondering what he'd done wrong this time, as he tried not to act like a baby and allow his mum to see him crying.

Sam suddenly remembered. 'Oh! Gosh! Alfie looked up. I forgot I have to meet Tom's mum for a coffee. She rushed upstairs saying, get ready Alfie, quickly, please'. Alfie had dressed himself well. She helped brush his hair and straightened his school tie. It was always knotted, so all Alfie had to do was to put it over his head. She saw his sad face.

'I'm not angry with you love, mum is just so tired, give me a smile.'

Alfie obliged, and Sam couldn't help herself but give him a big, sloppy, kiss.

'Mum!' he squealed, as he rubbed the kiss away with the back of his hand, taking Sam's lipstick along with it.

'You look nice'. Sam smiled, knowing that a touch of makeup and her best clothes made a vast difference to her appearance.

The mums dropped the boys off and drove to the nearest coffee shop, ordering hot drinks on the way in and introducing themselves again, laughing as they shook hands. To Sam's surprise they got on well, both apologising for their son's previously bad behaviours, but saying that they now seem to be good friends.

'I must have Alfie over after school, soon', said Kate, then suddenly added Congratulations!'

'Thanks, said Sam. I can't believe how tired and grumpy I am. I don't remember being like this with Alfie.'

'How far gone are you?'

'Twenty weeks scan due next week, said Sam, but I feel so big already.' Kate laughed.

'You look great, not expecting twins by any chance?' Sam did not react but was glad that they found plenty to talk about although nothing in particular until Kate suddenly said, I'm a single mum. We lived with my Dad, but I decided to move away after he died, so it's nice that Tom has Alfie for a friend'.

'Do you intend staying in this area?'

'Yes. I hope to find a job, but of course it has to be around Tom. I was thinking of their school, but I really don't like their Head too much.'

'Me neither', said Sam, so let's hope our sons can keep out

of trouble. Both mums' left happily saying that they'll have to meet up again.

Sam gave Carol a ring when she got home. She told her about Alfie seeing Tom's Grandad and how that had led to them fighting in the playground.

'Alfie fighting, I can't believe it, she giggled, your little charmer?'

'It's not funny, but that's how Kate and I have become friends; we were called into the Head's office to sort things out. We both agreed that the school should have dealt with it, or given us the chance to deal with the incident ourselves, rather than the fuss of calling us in. We backed each other up. Seriously Carol, I want to help Alfie with all of this. I think he doesn't know when to say what he sees and hears and when to keep quiet. I can tell that sometimes his words come out before he grasps what is actually happening to him. I want to help him but I don't know how.'

'Sorry, said Carol. I didn't know you were worrying about him. Do you want to come over for lunch next week and we'll talk things through?'

Dave was having breakfast as Alfie came downstairs. 'Are you going to see Grace again?'

Both Sam and Dave were startled they still could not believe the casual manner in which Alfie spoke about the baby. Eventually they got their act together and smiled. 'Can I come' asked Alfie.

'It's a school day.'

'I can go in later.'

'You are already in trouble, said Sam, but we'll think

about it. In the meantime, eat your breakfast and get ready for school.' Alfie looked sad but said nothing.

'What do you think?' Dave thought that it was fine. They also checked with the hospital who agreed that Alfie could be there providing that the medical checks were completed first. Alfie was delighted to be told that he could go. He jumped up and down and then went over to hug each of them in turn. He kissed Sam's tummy and said, 'I'm coming to see you baby Grace.'

Dave sat in the waiting room with Alfie until a nurse came for them. Alfie was so engrossed in everything. He could hardly breathe, let alone speak, or indeed, make any sort of noise. When asked if Sam and Dave wanted to know the gender of the baby, they immediately said no. This was the only time Alfie was about to speak, but Dave put his hand over his mouth.

'Kids!' He smiled at the radiographer, she smiled back. The pair left the room. Sam soon joined them and there were big smiles all 'round. Getting home, there was another surprise for Alfie. He didn't have to go back to school.

'I'll send you in with a note in the morning saying you were unwell'.

Alfie smiled, 'Thanks'.

'I won't make it a habit', said Sam. It's a one off.'

'Can I change?'

'Yes'.

Alfie delightfully went upstairs to change out of his uniform. Dave drew out a chair at the dining table inviting Sam to sit down. The kettle had just boiled. Soon tea and toast was on the table which Dave covered in lashings of butter for himself. 'You're taking your time'.

'That's because I'm not going in.' Sam looked surprised and shocked, as Alfie appeared in his jeans and jumper.

'All home together, that's super', he said. They did have a good day, although Sam dozed through most of it. This gave Dave more of a push to keep forging forward with his work ideas, and tomorrow he would put his thoughts and suggestions before his men.

Dave and his men met the following morning as he proceeded to tell them about his ideas and suggestions regarding breaking away from the Company and going it alone. Dave explained what he had in mind, which was to be salesmen just as they were, but to buy and sell on the Internet.

'How?' they asked.

'Simple, we look and see which items are most purchased; we check the Internet, find the Company's or individual's selling the products customers' require. We order, sell and post the items to them. It takes organizing, that's all. We order cheap and sell expensive, let that be our moto! In the meantime, we carry on working as usual and no one need know, agreed?' The three others nodded; they were too shocked to speak. Dave sat up late that night getting ideas ready, making notes, drawing charts. He felt in a way that it was almost a student's project, but of course it would be worked on a huge scale. A month later he met the men in a pub at lunchtime. They seemed interested, but nervous. Two of them had wives and children to think about; they had to earn a reasonable wage.

'Me too,' said Dave. I have a baby coming along and that's why I want to do this. Yes, I also need money, but I want to spend more time at home with my wife and family. At present I am checked on by management constantly. I get lectures on profit and loss, moans on having to meet sale targets and much more, all a thorn in my side, this way I am hoping that we can all work together, not as boss and workers but as friends. Let's start by looking for four items to buy and sell on the Internet. Let's do a little maths test. Check buying price of item and highest selling price, add on postage, and so on. Let's see what all three of you can come up with by next month, and how the change of working differently feels to all of you. How does that sound?'

Looking at each other Pete said. 'We'll give it a try and see what happens.'

'That's all I can ask for', said Dave.

Waiting for another month was a strain on Dave, but they had to carry on as normal in their present jobs. Dave checked on the sales targets and the men were hitting them; he'd just have to put up with the other moans. He hoped it wouldn't be for too much longer.

The following meeting was most successful.

Dave was to co-ordinate the whole business. 'I can handle everything if we form and register as a small Company said Dave. I would deal with everyone's legal matters covering their taxes, insurances, wages and all legal affairs he told the men. I have now completed an accountancy course and will keep looking for any other suitable courses which could help me move the Business forward. I will cross all the 'T's' and dot all the 'I's making sure each of us are safe and secure in our working lives.' When Bob spoke of wanting to continue with deliveries and they all agreed, he reassured them that any added expenses would always be covered by the Company. The men liked Dave's method of problem solving. They liked his willingness to talk, discuss and gain a conclusion. 'What I want is a successful business' Dave continued. For this to be achieved we all have to be open and honest at all times. I would agree to any of you looking at the books, if ever and whenever you feel the need. Wages will also be discussed openly. I don't want any one of you disgruntled about anything, or feel that as a Business Partner you are not being respected or not been taken seriously. This is the only way I feel that we can all be treated fairly and in turn this Business Agreement can percolate into a Business Friendship.

Chapter 23

The day soon came around for Sam to have lunch with Carol. She wondered if she'd come up with any new ideas on how someone can help Alfie understand what is happening to him during his psychic phases of seeing and hearing things beyond what's considered to be the norm. Sam had done some research and found there were other children like Alfie but didn't know if there were any nearby. Talking about psychic abilities still seemed a closed shop. She asked Jade about it after one of her circle meetings. Jade said that nobody talked about psychic children also known as Star children. 'If you know of other children like your son, I have the training required to teach them. I am also affiliated to the Spiritualist Organizations and Churches approval.

It was while Carol and Sam were talking about Alfie that Sam said. 'I didn't think to mention it to Jade at the time, but after doing platform work couldn't the mediums' just mention that if anyone in the congregation has a gifted child needing guidance that Jade could help them? Getting good, aren't I? She said, looking proud. Platform work, mediums, gifted child, guiding them, oh! I'm getting good.'

'You are enjoying your Spiritual journey; I can see that.'

Carol didn't have much to say about herself, so Sam asked. What news do you have for me?

'I have been looking into how much this house is worth. I've had a survey on this and Tanya's flat, she flinched in mentioning Tanya's name. I haven't decided upon anything, but I do think the flat will be a good move for me.'

'Really?'

'Yes. No garden to worry about and this is far too big. I found Tanya's flat to be quite cosy in comparison and I liked that. We'll see.'

'You wouldn't want to marry again?' asked Sam.

'Never thought about it, still don't.'

'That's a shame. I'm sure you have a lot to offer someone.' Carol simply shrugged her shoulders as if dismissing the thought. She was however, delighted to hear that all was well with Sam's baby and about Alfie going along to see the scan.

'Was he ok?'

'Engrossed, and well behaved, until the nurse asked if we wanted to know the baby's gender. Who knows what he was about to say, but Dave put his hand across his mouth so as nothing could come out.

Carol was in fits of laughter. 'I'm so glad to be your friend Sam. We were meant to meet and share our lives, mine, as little as it may be.'

'Nonsense! Interrupted Sam. You introduced me to Spiritualism and now I'm flying with it. Maybe Alfie will too, one day.'

'Dave will kill me, Carol laughed. Getting you involved

with the unknown the deceased and then both you and Alfie wanting to take that life further.'

Carol dunked the tea bag into the cup, offering Sam another sandwich. 'Not like Queenie and her teapot and tinkling teacups' she smiled.

'Dave told me about a dream he had said Sam. He said that it felt as if he was in another land and he believed that he was. I teased him about other worlds coming to visit Alfie and myself, whereas he goes to visit them.'

'What did he say?'

'Nothing! He turned a whiter shade of pale and rushed off to work.'

Carol laughed saying, 'I'm so glad that I know such a lovely family.'

Alfie had been to Tom's after school. Kate said that the boys' were fine and that Alfie is very polite. Sam thanked Kate as they left for home. Alfie was happy telling Sam about the toys Tom has and what they did and had to eat and drink. Suddenly he asked with sadness in his voice. 'Why doesn't Tom have a Dad?

'I don't know', said Sam. But it should make you feel lucky that you have yours around.'

'I do, it's great' replied Alfie, grinning. Homework done, time spent in playing and reading and Alfie was ready for bed when Dave walked in.

'Dad!' He ran over and jumped up at him. I'm glad you are here', he said.

'So am I' said Dave, wondering what was going on this

time. Sam told Alfie to go and play while Dave had his meal, after which Dave put him to bed.

'What was that all about?' he asked Sam later.

'Nothing to worry about. We were talking about Tom not having a Dad around, so I told him that he should be pleased that you are here for us. I guess that he was trying to show you how grateful and happy he is that you are around by jumping all over you.' Dave just smiled.

Relaxing together Dave said to Sam. 'I've been working on an idea with the three guys who work under me. I've been trying to convince them that we should form our own Company, they are all thinking about it'.

'Oh!' said Sam surprised. What's brought this on?'

'I'm fed up with Management checking up on me when I'm doing a perfectly good job and I think with these guys we could be a success. We will of course have to diverse, somewhat, but as I say we're working on it. The most important part is that I want to work from home and I think this will work out fine. I want to be with you and the baby and I could help Alfie as well, even do the school run and so-on.

'Why didn't you mention this before?'

'I wanted to see what the guys thought.'

'What do they think?'

'They are all for it, although nervous said Dave. We all have to make sure we earn enough money, but I know we can, providing everything is run smoothly. Bob wants to still be on the road so if he can make that work that's good for everyone. The idea is to buy and sell via the Internet, but we're still meeting and discussing further details. Don't want me home then?' He asked as an afterthought.

'No, love, sorry! It'll be good but I don't want Alfie to play up about having to go to school if the three of us are all at home.'

Dave touched her tummy and kissed her. 'I'll make sure all is good with Alfie.' The next moment Sam was sound asleep with her head resting on Dave's shoulder.

Sam's GP check-up showed her blood pressure to be slightly high and when questioned she remarked how tired she was and how she fell asleep so often. He gave her a prescription for iron tablets saying she might be slightly anaemic. Hearing this, Dave wanted to be home more often. He checked into this and learnt that he had some leave days owing and decided to take them soon, as Sam was seven months pregnant and could do with more rest.

Dave had a final meeting with the men, by which point they were ready to break away from their present situation and start up their own Company. Dave was excited, the men were ready for a new adventure, and the present Company Boss was pulling his hair out when four of his employees handed in their notice all at once.

In the mean while Sam carried on as usual, although feeling like a whale. Alfie often laughed as she waddled back, forth, side-ways. 'I was like this with you too, you know.' Alfie giggled even more. Dave booked off the day's owing to him. They shopped for baby items and they put Alfie's cot up in the spare room and made the room look fresh and clean without having to redecorate. Sam added bits and pieces to it including a Rocking Chair now it looked more like a Nursery than a spare room.

One Saturday afternoon Dave called out that he was taking Alfie shopping. 'Don't spend too much money Sam called back. We have to see how your new business goes.' Dave smiled, as Alfie excitedly called, 'Bye Mum' as they both walked out the door. Sam went upstairs to tidy Alfie's very messy room but did not get very far as she felt exhausted again, she quickly paid a visit to the bathroom and then headed to their bedroom. She lay on top of the covers with a nearby throw-over covering her and fell asleep.

Alfie and Dave returned home with Alfie carrying a Giant Teddy Bear bigger than himself.

'Mum!' he shouted. Disappointed, he looked in all the rooms downstairs for Sam. Suddenly jerking awake she found herself feeling wet and uncomfortable. She realized that her waters had gone. Alfie was standing beside her, ashen faced and in shock. Trying to keep her voice even she said, 'Get Dad love' as Alfie dashed downstairs.

'Dad! Mum needs you.'

Dave flew up the stairs two at a time as Sam was already phoning the hospital from her mobile. Taking Alfie into the hallway Dave said. 'Put some toys and drawing things into your backpack. Go for a wee and wait for me in your bedroom. Alfie did has he was told, still looking dazed. Dave sat beside Sam reassuring and cuddling her. The ambulance was on its way as Sam had hurriedly explained to Dave what was happening. Alfie saw the flashing blue lights as Dave went to answer the front door. He stood at his bedroom window, watching, numbed. While the paramedics carefully placed Sam in the ambulance Dave went back upstairs to Alfie.

'Mum's going to be fine, we need to go. Have you got your bag?' Alfie nodded. Dave had Sam's bag with him as he locked up the house. The ambulance had just left as Alfie and Dave got into the car and headed for the hospital.

Sam was already in the Labour Ward by the time Dave parked the car and found the Maternity Unit. They were directed to a waiting area where Dave began pacing the floor as Alfie sat on a chair swinging his legs. Dave happened to place his hand in his jacket pocket only to find Sam's mobile in it. He had no idea how it got there, but it was a blessing in disguise. He went to a nearby desk and asked that if he could get someone to sit with Alfie and would it be ok for him to go and stay with Sam, as planned. He did not want Alfie to feel left out, or alone so returning to him he said.

'If Carol can come and sit with you, would you mind if I went and stayed with Mum?' Alfie looking pale said quietly,

'OK'. Dave ruffled his hair as he looked for Carol's mobile number she was at home and happy to meet them at the hospital. Father and Son sat and waited, Dave with his arm around Alfie. They saw Carol walking down the hallway, as Dave noticed that seeing Carol seemed to cheer Alfie up right away. They sat together for a while, Alfie sitting on Carol's lap. Dave thanked her for coming, then rushed off to spend time with Sam and to welcome their new baby.

Alfie talked to Carol about the Giant Teddy Bear they'd bought for Grace and how they had presents for Mum, too. He talked quietly to Carol about how he'd run upstairs to find his Mum and she was in bed and the sheets were wet. She told him 'to go and get Dad' he said.

'You were very grown up and brave' Carol said. The water was because the baby grows in a bag of water and when the bag breaks open the water comes out, then the baby is more ready to be born.' Alfie stretched his arms upwards and backwards placing them around Carol's neck. She tickled him under an arm, just to ease the tension. It worked; Alfie giggled. He put his arms back down and stood up.

In time, Dave rushed over to them. 'Mum and Baby are both doing well he said breathlessly. Grace is with us. Alfie, she is so pretty! He looked at Carol. She was even born gracefully. She slid out, and then moved her arms and legs as if dancing on ice!'

'Congratulations!' said Carol. She gave Dave a hug and kiss on his cheek and struggling managed to pick Alfie up and gave him a kiss too.

'Can we see Mum and Grace?' They sat down again, Dave in the middle.

'We can see Mum in time, when they move her to a ward', he looked at Carol. Grace has been taken to a Special place where they can keep her warm, she is doing well, but is a bit cold.' Carol knew what Dave meant. Grace was in the Neo-Natal Unit in an incubator.

'I could do with a drink, would either of you like something asked Carol?'

'I'll get it' said Dave being the perfect gentleman.

'You spend some time with him', she glanced at Alfie. She got herself and Dave a cup of coffee from the machine and got Alfie a hot drinking chocolate. They were sipping their drinks when a nurse came to take them to see Sam saying that she was very tired. Dave and Alfie went in first. Alfie seemed a bit afraid. 'Are you alright love?' Dave picked Alfie up and sat him on the bed beside his mum. He took her hand and held it.

'I want a big kiss' she said, leaning as far forward as she could manage. Alfie also leant forward as he placed his arms around her neck and kissed her. 'That's better' she said. Dave soon realized that Sam needed to lie down again. He lifted Alfie under his arms and sat him back down on the bed.

'You'll see baby Grace soon' Sam said to Alfie. He looked in the direction of the Baby Unit and said. 'I can see her; she is in like a plastic box and has a pink cap on. She says 'Hello! Alfie'.

'Hello! Grace', he said to the air. Sam and Dave glanced at each other, but Alfie seemed more himself and less worried.

It was Carol's turn next. She leant into Sam, holding her shoulders and kissing her cheek. 'Congratulations!'

'Thank you so much Carol', she said. Stay with my family tonight. Dave does know where things are in the house, and how to change sheets', she smiled shyly. Mine ended up wet, I'm afraid.'

'Yes, your Son told me. I explained that the baby lays in a sack of water, hope you don't mind. It seemed to calm him down when he knew how the water got there.'

'Stay', she said again, falling asleep while holding Carol's hand. Carol slid her hand out of Sam's and left her side.

The three finally left the hospital, with Dave trying to get Carol to stay with them, but she decided to go home. The spare room is spare no-more thought Carol, smiling to herself. Dave said he would phone her the following day.

Dave woke up to find Alfie beside him. He was so glad that Grace had been born while he was on leave, especially under the circumstances of Sam being rushed into hospital. Father and Son ate breakfast together and were relaxing at home. Alfie was playing with his Lego when he suddenly said, 'Baby Grace is small, isn't she?' Dave went over to him.

'A little bit but she is doing fine.'

'I think Mum will be home before her.' Dave tried to keep calm.

'Why do you say that Alfie?'

'Grace told me, but she isn't sure. The doctors were talking softly, she couldn't hear properly.'

Dave lost it. He stood Alfie up and shook his shoulders. 'Stop making things up, he yelled. Grace is a day old; she doesn't know what is happening, never mind telling you about it.' Alfie burst into tears. Dave grabbed him and pulled him into his body as he knelt down at Alfie's level. Alfie cried on his shoulder. Dave felt terrible.

'Sorry' he said. I didn't mean to shout or pull you about. Do you forgive me?' Alfie pulled away and went back to his Lego. Dave wished that Carol was with them, she seemed to know Alfie better than he did.

'Shall we go to the park, Alfie?' Alfie shrugged his shoulders. How about if we see if Carol wants to go with us, after which we can all go together to visit Mum. Dave phoned

Carol but there was no reply. Just then the doorbell rang. Alfie jumped up and looked at Dave.

'Go ahead' he said and then watched as Carol stood there hidden by big bags and gift-wrapped presents.

'Is that you Alfie?' she teased as she put some of the packages down just inside the door. Dave helped by moving them so that Carol could actually step into the house. There was a big hug around Carol's waist from Alfie making Dave once again feel as if he wasn't in tune with Alfie in a Fatherly way. They had coffee together and chatted. Alfie soon saw his name on some of the items. He took a wrapped box over to Carol as together they unwrapped it.

'Wow!' said Alfie. Inside was a Book about having a new baby sister, plus balloons and streamers and a plaque with Alfie's name on it.

'I thought we could decorate your bedroom with these, she fiddled with the streamer, that's if your Dad doesn't mind, and then we can do Baby Grace's room before she comes home.' Alfie jumped in glee pulling Carol toward his bedroom. She looked over her shoulder at Dave who mouthed, 'Thank you.'

They went out to lunch together, then to the park and then to visit Sam. There was no Grace by her bed and Sam looked withdrawn. After greeting them she asked Dave to put Alfie on her bed telling him that's it lovely to see him while giving him hugs and kisses again. Sam then said to Alfie, 'I'm sorry that you can't see Baby Grace yet.'

'That's OK Mum' he said. I already told Dad that Grace

is small and she will have to stay here, you will come home before her.' Dave nodded.

'Sorry I was angry with you', again he ruffled Alfie's hair. I was just sad to hear you say that.' Alfie looked at Sam and Carol in a strange way as if to say. When is Dad going to believe what I tell him? Sam and Carol soon worked out that Alfie and Grace were talking to each other telepathically.

'I saw Grace earlier,' said Sam. She is getting bigger' she looked at Alfie then at the grownups. She's feeding slowly, but she will get there.' Carol was desperate to see her but didn't say anything as she didn't want Alfie to feel left out. They talked together for a while longer and then Dave and Alfie went to the Neo-Natal Unit to visit Grace. Her beautiful blue eyes were open slightly, her face was small and round, she was so cute. She moved her arms and legs in what looked like some-sort of a rendition of the ballet Swan Lake.

'Would you like to hold her?' The nurse asked Dave. She took Grace out of her incubator and handed her to Dave. He moved to a large chair, took Grace, and sat comfortably cuddling her as Farther and Daughter looked at each other in awe. 'Do you know why she was born early?' he asked.

'I can get a doctor to come and talk to you' was the nurse's reply.

'Yes, please' said Dave, firmly.

Sam had asked to go to Unit as well but was shocked to see Dave talking to a doctor as she was being wheeled along the corridor. The doctor passed her on his way out.

'What's wrong?' she asked Dave while Carol walked across the unit to join them.

'Nothing. I just wanted to speak to a doctor.'

'Why?'

'I needed to know that I hadn't t neglected you in anyway Sam, but he reassured me on that, saying that he'll come back and talk to us later. You were always tired perhaps I should have done more to help you.'

Sam eased herself out of her wheelchair and walked slowly towards Dave, as Alfie skipped over and took her hand. 'Are you allowed to do that?

'I do walk, you know', she said causally as together with Alfie they stood behind Dave as Sam causally hung her arm around Dave's neck reaching down to touch Grace. Carol watched from afar but now rushed over at this beautiful sight, she was the first person to take a family photograph with Baby Grace included. Upon seeing the doctor return-ing, she suggested that she take Alfie for a walk

so that they could talk in private. Reading and recheck-ing Grace's chart he said. 'I'm afraid I can't give you a good reason for her early delivery, sometimes these things just happen. He looked at the chart again and then at Grace. She is beginning to feed better. I can see Mrs. James has been both breast feeding and expressing milk for her, her suck-ing action is improving and so she seldom has a tube feed now, unless absolutely necessary. She has always breathed on her own, as you know, so there is no problem there. She is putting on weight, slowly, but is still cold. Her body temper-ature needs to learn how to control itself, but it will all come together in the end.

'They are all so clever and nice here', said Sam as the doctor walked away. We have nothing to worry about, but I am due to come home tomorrow and I hate the thought of leaving Grace.' A tear appeared in her eye. She has to mature a bit more before she can come home.' They looked at their daughter with love and appreciation.

Carol returned with Alfie and said a quick goodbye to everyone, Sam thanking her for all the lovely presents she had bought for the children. 'The children Sam said again, sounds strange!'

'You know, she said to Sam you and your family mean so much to me. I get so much love and pleasure being around all of you.'

'It's official then, said Sam. Would you be Godmother to both my children?'

'Have you spoken to Dave?' '

Don't worry about him', laughed Sam. He hasn't a clue about these things. Please say yes'.

Of-course. I would love to.

'Can I tell Queenie?'

'Sure. Give her our love'.

Dave looked on dumb-founded, as Sam knew he would.

Carol felt a weird sensation around them. She took a second look and saw Tanya standing beyond Sam's bed, smiling. Carol smiled back Tanya faded away.

Alone with Alfie Dave reminded him that he had school the following day. Dave got Alfie to school fresh, clean and happy. He was proud of himself and spent the day tidying around and worked further on developing his business. He had told the men to think up a Business Name and Logo so he thought he'd better check for any messages. He turned on his laptop to find Congratulation messages from his colleagues, alongside a suggested Business Name and Logo from one of them. Dave couldn't help but smile, and then he laughed out loud. This, he knew was in reference to him saying that he wanted them to work as friends rather than Boss and Workers. The Company name suggested was: In the Company of Friends. The Logo was a drawing of a Circle of men shaking hands.

Dave cooked a meal of fish fingers, chips and peas for dinner. Alfie had said that it was his favourite. The evening went quickly for them and Dave missed not seeing Sam again. Carol did offer to sit with Alfie but both Sam and Dave agreed that there was no need. In the end however, Carol phoned Dave and asked if he would mind if she visited Sam instead, he happily agreed.

Chapter 24

Alfie had a good day at school and came home with stickers for being really good. He couldn't explain exactly what that meant, but he got lots of praise and cuddles anyhow. Did you tell anyone about Grace?' Asked Dave.

'Yes, I told Tom, but I didn't tell him that she was small and in a special place.' His voice sounded quiet and sad.

'That's ok said Dave. We can ask Mum to ring Tom's mum when she is ready'.

Alfie went to his school bag and got out his reading book. 'It's a new one' he said proudly.

'Then let's see how you do.' To Dave's surprise Alfie flew through the pages in one go. His reading was perfect and Dave was really impressed. 'That's wonderful! Do you want some more ice cream?' he asked when Alfie's book was safely tucked away. Father and Son sat at the dining table and ate extra ice cream, feeling like two naughty boys as they chuckled together.

'Have you opened your other presents from Carol?' Dave asked.

'No. I wanted to wait until Mum got home.' He sounded as if he was missing her, so it was good that she rang up later that night to say that she would be home the following day.

Alfie was still awake and went to bed happy as Dave told Sam that they were looking forward to it.

Sam and Dave were upset to leave Grace behind, so it was with very mixed emotions that they left the hospital. Upon being at home for a while Sam seemed some-what restless. Dave could hear her, moving from room to room. He was torn by wanting to follow her or giving her some space. In the end he left her alone. She came down with tears in her eyes saying how beautiful the huge Teddy Bear looks sitting in a corner of Grace's bedroom and how nice it was of Carol to help Alfie decorate his.

'Love his name plaque on his door too' she said as tears ran down her cheeks. We'll have to decorate Grace's room before she comes home. I saw the streamers lying in her cot. Dave gave her a big cuddle.

'Grace will be home soon' he said gently.

When Sam was ready, she made arrangements to meet both Carol and Kate. Her energy was slowly returning and she wanted to be there for her own family once Grace was home.

Instead of just meeting up with Carol, she asked her if she would like to see Grace again.

Carol was enthusiastic about it and Dave didn't mind, and so they did just that. Carol was so overcome by seeing Grace that she broke down.

'Anyone would think that you are her Mum,' laughed Sam.

'I wouldn't mind at all, said Carol. Oh! She is beautiful, like an Angel. Just look at her round cherubic face and sparkling blue eyes!' When Sam cuddled Grace, she realized that not only had she grown in length but she felt heavier too. The nurse confirmed that she was right. Sam handed her over to Carol for a cuddle. She looked at Grace lovingly, as the nurse asked to speak to Sam.

'Nothing to worry about' she began, seeing the concern on Sam's face. I just wanted to tell you that Grace seems somehow different, special. She seems to follow people's voices and understands what they are saying to her. Every one of us who has cared for her sees all of her attributes as she looks directly and intently into our eyes, we wanted to let you know, hope you don't mind.'

'Not at all said Sam. I'm glad she makes you and your colleagues' feel that way for you must be very special people to cope with these', she looked around, tiny babies and see life and death before your eyes.'

'Yes, it is difficult, heart breaking even, but we learn to cope and hopefully it teaches us to appreciate life more, including all its ups and downs' she said. Sam looked at Carol; she was totally engrossed in Grace. Sam and Carol sat together again as Sam gave Grace one last cuddle before they left the Special Unit. Carol was very quiet on the return walk to the waiting area. Sam asked if she was alright.

'Yes, just thinking'. Sam could hear the emotion in her voice. Some of those babies were so tiny, needing so much equipment; Miracles must happen in that unit.'

'It does, said Sam. That lovely nurse Lucy was just telling me all about it.' Sam didn't elaborate, but she did ask Carol over for a coffee as together they decorated Grace's bedroom.

There was laughter and tears at not knowing exactly when Grace would be home but their time together was still a happy one. They came down to have coffee with Dave. Sam thanked her again for the presents for Grace, saying she loved the name plaque she choose and also the tiny outfits.

'I hope they are ok. I told the lady in the shop she was born early she said, 'these should fit, they are made especially.' Sam had brought a couple down to show to Dave.

'They are beautiful', said Dave.

Carol left to give them some time together before returning later to stay with Alfie while Sam and Dave once again visited Grace in hospital.

'What would we do without you,' said Dave.

'You'll do just fine' said Carol, smiling.

Alfie finally opened his last presents with Carol. He somehow never found the right time to open them in front of his parents, but he was pleased with Carol being there for him. He gave her a big hug as she said. 'I could get used to this'.

Two days later Grace came home. There was total enjoyment and love all around. Alfie loved sitting holding Grace. Often it seemed as if, once again they were reading each other's mind.

Dave did his share of attending to Grace through the night. She strived on the love and attention which she was receiving. Alfie asked if Tom could come over to meet Grace. It was arranged for Tom and Kate to visit and after their meal the boys went off to play. Sam and Kate caught up on their news, as Grace lay beside them in her swing cradle. Kate told

Sam that she had applied for a Dinner Supervisor Position at the School. 'With that job' she said. There is very little chance of me coming into contact with Mr. Brown and hopefully something better would come along soon.'

Sam hadn't seen Queenie in a while so out of the blue she asked Dave about taking the whole family to meet her.

'That's fine, but wouldn't it make more sense for her to come here? One of us will have to drive her around.'

That's ok. I'll do it.'

They asked Carol too and she was happy to drive Queenie around with her and so they made the visit for a weekend.

Queenie right away became part of the family. She cooed over Grace and played games with Alfie and told Dave what a wonderful husband and father he was. Everyone was happy. Alfie once again surprised everyone by saying to Queenie 'You met Tanya, didn't you? Tanya is Carol's sister'. Sam was about to tell him off, but Queenie stopped her by placing her hand on Sam's arm.

'It is alright, dear', she said. Queenie looked at Alfie. How do you know that? She asked. Alfie came back with another question. 'Am I right?'

'Yes,' said Queenie. Alfie looked at Queenie more earnestly.

'I don't know how I know. Things just come into my head.'

'Well! That's good' said Queenie but sometimes you can tell people what you know, and other times it is better to keep quiet'.

'Mum told me that he said. When she was very angry with me.'

'Oh!' said Queenie. You will learn these things as you get older, or she thought, maybe you will find someone who can teach you.'

'Can you teach me?'

'No dear I can't', she said almost in regret.

'Well, I hope we find someone who can, because I keep getting into trouble.' They all laughed as Alfie went to Grace and said. 'It's just us for now Grace'. The adults looked at each other in shock as Alfie went back to his Lego as if the whole conversation never existed. Queenie gave Alfie some money as she was leaving.

'Thank you' he said.

'Are you going to buy some toys? She asked. Alfie thought for a moment.

'Carol bought me a book about having a new baby sister which I really like. Maybe we can look for a book which tells me how I know things.' Queenie drew him into her waist and hugged him tightly. 'You are clever' she said.

'I can't breathe' mumbled Alfie. You are squashing me.' Queenie let go as Alfie stepped away taking in a deep breath and breathing out loudly.

'That's better' he said. Everyone laughed as his face lost its redness and returned to its normal colour.

When the house was quiet again Sam and Dave told Alfie how proud they were of him. He handed his mum the money which Queenie had just given him. 'If you see a book like the one I spoke about, would you buy it for me?'

'Don't' worry love, Sam said. We will sort you out.

Dave's business began to take off. Bob was happy to use

his own small van for deliveries. Their Logo looked good on his van. They all worked hard and the business profited. Dave was easy going both with himself and the Company employees, so they all worked their own hours around the clock. He took an online Business Management course which brought him up to date with certain issues and also boosted his confidence and abilities which meant he was able to push the Company on. The men became more like friends as they held meetings in pubs, coffee shops and each other's homes and so their families also became entwined for the good of all.

Chapter 25

Sam still went to her Circle meetings and to the Spiritual Church, sometimes on her own, other times with Carol. The thought of Alfie asking for a book to learn from was never far from her mind. She asked Jade if she could help Alfie but she didn't want to take on only one child.

Sam was out one morning with Grace in her pram. A stranger walked alongside and looked at Grace, saying, 'She looks like an Angel'.

'Yes, people do say that' said Sam smiling as the lady rushed by. Later, she found a note in the pram. It contained the title of a book and its author she immediately looked it up on the Internet and found it, and then scolded herself for not thinking about the Internet before, especially in view of Dave's new business. On the other hand, she wondered if this was a form of synchronization where people who are supposed to connect meet through outside influences. The book was written and designed especially for children with their own exercises to learn from under supervision. However, the book came their way was irrelevant. What was important was that Alfie wanted and needed it. It was ordered that night and arrived the following day.

Dave was busy with work as Grace dozed in her cot. Sam

was tidying around the house. It seemed so full of everything. Toys, clothes, bottles, nappies, she sometimes felt stressed out looking at the chaos, but was happy at the same time. She watched Dave moving around trying to find a space somewhere to settle with his laptop. The dining table often seemed cluttered so he would wonder into their bedroom either sitting on the bed with work papers surrounding him, or trying to balance his laptop on a tiny bedside table. Sam felt sorry for him. One day when they sat down for a quiet moment together, she asked him. 'Are you still happy working from home?'

'I love it', he said. There was no doubt in his voice whatsoever.

'You always seem pushed out there is not one place where you can settle in anymore.' Dave sipped his coffee. 'I love working from home. I can look at my beautiful wife and daughter whenever I want to. Alfie likes me being around too. I'm beginning to understand him better now. Space is a bit tight I must admit it would be nice to spread out. I'd love to have a proper office space where I can have a white board and track the day's schedule more efficiently amongst other things, but I don't want to work from anywhere else rather than home'.

'So, Sam said. Now might be the time to think about moving. I love having you at home. Alfie loves you doing the school run, Grace is getting used to you, we just need more space.'

'But you didn't want to move'.

'Things change Dave. It would be nice not to move too far

and keep Alfie in the same school. We need to look into it, what do you think? We would be moving not as a status symbol but out of comfort and necessity.'

Dave gave Sam a cuddle. 'Let's look into it together' he grinned, as Grace was stirring, ready for a feed.

Alfie had spent days mentioning his up-coming birthday. Dave and Sam played it down keeping him on his toes. Finally, Dave said. 'Would you like a birthday party?'

'No! I'd like to go ice skating.' Once again, his parents were taken aback.

'You've never been,' said Sam.

'That's why I want to go. It looks like fun. You watch that programme every week, Mum.'

'You'll have to learn from the beginning. No falling about like your Dad and I used to.'

'Did you used to go?'

'A long time ago,' said Dave.

'When we were young' said Sam, winking at Dave.

'Can we go? Alfie was already getting excited about the idea.

'I'll look into it. Do you want someone to go with you?'

'Tom'. Alfie bounced away towards Grace where he chatted away to her. Grace made baby noises in return, and everyone seemed happy and contended in the James' household. Sam looked into the idea of Children's ice skating and was thrilled that there was so much on offer. They had equipment for children to push around on the ice, giving them balance. This enabled them to skate and travel around the ice safely and confidently. They also offered birthday parties, but Sam wanted to have Alfie's at home. Dave said that he wanted to go on the ice with the boys. Sam couldn't wait to see that!

They booked up and even asked Tom if he would like to sleep over the night before, which was Alfie's suggestion. They had a camp bed which one of the boys' could sleep on in Alfie's room. Sam spoke to Kate about it and Tom was excited to be a big part of Alfie's sixth birthday.

Kate said to Sam. 'Thank you so much. Tom has never had such a close friend. I think Alfie is good for him.' She laughed embarrassed. 'After their dodgy start!'

Sam laughed too as she invited Kate along.

'You can come to the ice rink or the party at ours.' Kate opted for the party only. Carol was invited too, but Sam didn't give her a choice, after all she was the children's Godmother, even if only in name. She and Dave weren't particularly religious.

'You can meet us at the ice rink. Take your time; we are booked in for one hour.'

'I'll be there,' said Carol. I'm looking forward to it'.

Sam had invited Queenie to the house, so told her that either she or Dave would be over to get her as soon as they returned from the ice rink giving her a rough time.

'I'll be waiting, dear, no rush.'

'See you then' said Sam as she clicked off her mobile. While she was getting some of the food prepared Sam was thinking about the book she'd bought for Alfie from Queenie. She'd been wondering if she should ask Queenie to write a little something inside, that's why she hadn't given it to Alfie already.

The big day arrived and Sam had been watching the boys doing well on the ice, pushing the stabilizer and talking as they moved around the rink. She had to look harder to find Dave, but there he was, away from other people skating fairly confidently. He went back and forth for a short distance and then surprised her by doing little circles on the spot with his hands folded across his chest. She was impressed. She talked to Grace in her arms and pointed to Dave as Alfie skated up to them. Grace made little chuckling noises as Alfie leant over the barrier and pecked her on the cheek, then going off again. Sam thought what Alfie did was so cute that she nearly melted on the spot. Looking around, she found Dave again, he must have seen what Alfie had done for he came over and kissed Sam quickly on the lips and Grace on the forehead.

Sam shouted to Dave over the music. 'She's getting heavy, pointing to Grace. I'm going to have a seat.'

Sam was surprised to see Carol at the table, and even more shocked to see a man with her. She stopped and watched as they talked but Grace was now getting really heavy.

'Sorry' she said sitting down. She's getting heavier by the minute.'

'Here! Let me', said Carol taking Grace from her. Grace was relaxed and happy on Carol's lap.

'This is Ben. Ben Sam'.

They shook hands as Ben stood up. 'Hello!' said Sam.

'Ben asked if he could sit here,' said Carol. You saved your seats, the rest seemed taken.'

'I'll go'. Sam looked at Carol.

Carol did not say anything so Sam said.

'That's fine Ben stay. They are still on the ice.'

The conversation seemed to stop. Carol looked and played with Grace.

'Got someone here?' asked Sam, to ease the quietness around the table.

'My son,' said Ben. Actually, I'd better chase him up. I thought he'd be finished by now.' He excused himself and left. Sam watched. He walked over to a woman standing nearby and took a backpack from her and called to a boy still skating.

The buzzer then sounded and it was time for Alfie and Tom to leave.

'Can I leave Grace with you Carol?'

'Of course,'

Sam smiled. She's distracted. I wonder what went on there.

Returning, Sam was surprised to see Ben back at their table talking to Carol, his son beside him. Sadly, they were leaving, I could have invited them back to ours thought Sam there's plenty of food.

'Alright? Asked Sam while taking Grace back. She noticed how flushed Carol looked. She bent down and strapped Grace into her car seat.

'I'll get that' said Dave as Sam stood up. He picked up the car seat by the handle as they headed for the car. Carol walked ahead of them saying nothing, much to Sam's surprise. When they got to the car park all she said was. 'I'll see you at yours' as she headed for her own car. Sam was baffled by Carol's behaviour. 'What do you make of that?'

'What?' said Dave.

'Carol'.

'She's gone to her car.'

'I know that!' she said impatiently. Dave shrugged his shoulders. Sam didn't want to spoil the atmosphere so said nothing more. Men! she thought to herself. The boys' continued to talk and laugh and were still on a high, with plenty more surprises to come.

They were all settled indoors when Dave said. 'Shall I go and get Queenie?'

'I'll go,' said Carol.

'You relax,' said Dave.

'No please, I'd like to go'.

'But you ran Queenie around the last time'.

'I'll go!' said Carol firmly, already rummaging around in her handbag for her car keys. When she was gone Sam went up to Dave. 'See what I mean?' Dave's reply was a kiss.

Carol took time out on the drive over to Queenie's. She stopped the car, stood out in the open and took a deep breath. She was never a real smoker but now she craved for one, wondering why her nerves were so on edge. She knew that she already liked this man, but could not fathom out why, having spoken to him for only a short while. He told her that he was divorced and had a son and although Carol did not feel totally comfortable about this, she still gave him her mobile number. What on earth is drawing her to this man? Why on earth did she do that? Suddenly she remembered Queenie. She was losing track of time she'd better get on. Arriving, she noticed Queenie at the window. As they met, they gave each other a kiss on the cheek.

'Are you alright dear? You seem a bit hot?' Hot and bothered she thought, but all she said was that she'd been rushing around. Soon they were in the car and on their way back to Sam's. How Carol wished, for just this once, that she could go straight home. However, she did manage to hold herself together, even socializing with Kate, although Kate was doing most of the talking.

The house was quiet at last. Tom and Kate had left. Alfie was getting ready for bed; Grace was already in bed and Dave was driving Queenie home. Carol sat in the living room while Sam tidied the kitchen. She half expected Carol to say that she was going home too, but she just sat there. Suddenly, Sam saw Carol look into the corner of the room, following her gaze she was rewarded by seeing an outline of a man forming, he quickly took shape. Standing there, he smiled and waved at Carol. He said something, but Sam had no idea what as she looked at Carol again. She was now looking down at her hands laid in her lap.

'What is happening Carol?' Did you see him?' she asked.

'Carol! Shouted Alfie.

'I can't' she said. I just need to be alone.'

'Carol needs to go Alfie. I'll be up in a minute.' Sam understood that Carol had much thinking to do she truly did need time on her own. They said a quick goodbye and Carol drove away.

Sam rushed upstairs before Alfie could shout again. She didn't want Grace woken up. Alfie was sound asleep with the book which Queenie had now written in wrapped around the inside of his hand she gently prised it out. Not bedtime reading thought Sam. I'll call it a learning book and go through it with him. She explained this to him when he asked what had happened to his book. 'Psychic Kids is a learning book, she said. I'll keep it safe and we'll read and go through the exercises together over the weekends, ok?' Alfie nodded.

Time seemed to go quickly as Grace, grew and matured and was soon on the move. She bounced up and down while standing on people's laps and made more baby noises, she tried clapping her hands and loved being on the floor kicking and moving. She was nearly crawling already. Being on solid foods meant that Sam could take her out more and she generally had a drink and jar of baby food with her, so here they were at Carol's, Grace being safely propped up on a dinning chair, ready to be fed. They were used to this, as there was no room at Sam's for a highchair.

Dave, while they were out made much use of the dining table, spreading his work out. Sometimes he took the opportunity to have their monthly meeting at their home, but space was still a struggle.

This Saturday was a homely affair as Alfie played quietly and then moved on to entertain Grace. She giggled as they looked at her picture book together.

Dave called Sam over to the table, she was surprised to

see him looking at houses, and they causally looked at them together, this giving them an idea of what they could afford and in which nearby areas. They were looking at four bed-roomed houses, five bedroomed at a push, which would also give them a bigger garden. Taking out a new Mortgage or extending their present one would be necessary so they added those thoughts and figures into the equation. It was while they were doing this that Carol phoned.

'Sorry! I haven't been in touch for a while'.

'That's ok; I knew you would you ring when you were ready. How are you?'

'Good! I've made some plans and would like to talk to you about them. Can we meet for coffee?

They agreed to meet the following morning. Grace was happily sitting in her high buggy watching the world go by. Carol got the coffees and they settled down. Sam waited for Carol to speak, but it was a long time coming. In the end Sam said, 'Still seeing Ben?' 'Hmm... On and Off'.

'Was he part of your decision making?' She looked at Carol's face. She knew she was rushing her. 'Sorry, said Sam. I'll let you speak.'

'I saw John at the hospital.'

Did you? What happened?' asked Sam.

He smiled and waved and then said. 'Life is for living.' It made me realize, although it hurts, that moving out of this house will help me move on.'

Sam took Grace out of her buggy and gave her a teething rattle to chew on and play with. She hoped Carol would not be distracted, but she hated to leave her children without attention for too long no matter how well behaved they were being. As soon as Sam settled with Grace on her lap Carol leaned across the table and kissed her.

'Hello! Beautiful' she said. Grace giggled back, giving Carol her best baby smile.

'Can I hold her?'

'Of course.' Having Grace on her lap seemed to give Carol something to focus on, rather than looking straight into Sam's face across the table.

'I know you are interested in Ben and me. We've been out a few times. Lunches, dinners, even the pictures once. We get on really great, actually, but I never saw and still can't see another man in my life. I've told him this.' Carol took a deep breath. He says that is ok. We can stay as we are, but he still wants to keep seeing me.'

'That's good. You can do things your way.' Carol was back to shrugging her shoulders in that don't care attitude. Grace began getting restless, pretty soon she was crying. Sam looked at her watch. It was way past her mealtime.

'You'd better get her home,' said Carol. Sam wondered if Carol meant that she'd spoken enough.

'I've got baby food for her. I can stay, but if you need to go...

'Can you come to mine?' They paid and rushed off so as Grace could get fed.

At Carol's Sam propped Grace up safely on a dinning chair and fed her. Both had got used to this, there was no room for a highchair at home. Carol made coffee and began talking again. She looked around the house, her house.

'It's too big! I want to sell it and it's almost as if John is telling me just that by saying it's time to move on. I'm going to move into Tanya's old flat, mine now. Sam looked at her shocked. That's what I was thinking about. It has nothing at all to do with Ben but has a lot to do with you and your family.

'How?' Sam was taken aback.

'You can have this house if you want it. I've wasted enough money on paying council tax on Tanya's flat. I might as well use it. It's more than enough for me. I don't need to sell this house for the money; the flat is paid off, so it's all yours.'

'You can't just give your house away, Carol.'

'I can to you and yours. It's mine and I can do whatever I want with it.'

Sam nearly dropped Grace's food all down Carol's nice furniture; having just heard the sheer determination in Carol's voice.

You'll have to spend money on it anyway. I know it needs decorating which is good as you can do it to your own style. It's an old house, so I'm sure it needs lots of renovating as well. By now Sam was in shock. She'd finished feeding Grace and was wiping her hands and face with wet ones.

'Look! Carol said. I am not holding you to anything. We will always be friends, but just talk to Dave. It will save us both all the hassle of going through Estate Agents and others. The only real expense for both of us would be legal fees for the transfer of the house into your name. Why don't you come here as a family? Spend some time here next weekend.

You can have a proper look around. Alfie and Grace can play in the garden. Bring Alfie's football'. Carol smiled at Sam for the first time in ages and said not a word more about Ben. They gave each other the usual hug before leaving and having had Grace on her lap again Carol kissed her before handing her back to Sam. They waved as Sam pulled away.

When the children had gone to bed Sam told Dave all about her conversation with Carol.

'She's right in some ways you know. We will all save so much money by not getting Estate Agents and others involved, but of-course we will pay her whatever the house has been valued at. Be firm, she has to tell you what that is, or no deal, no matter how much we like the house. We could get it valued also, but again if Carol is happy with the price, then we won't need to pay out on getting one done. We can check what other houses in her area are selling for and do a Google map search for distance from Alfie's school, shops and so-on. We can also check Carol's actual house and it grounds. What do you think of the house?'

'I haven't seen much of it. The angle of the living room just gives you a glimpse of a large door leading into the garden but you can't see the garden from where we sit. The toilet is upstairs. You can see many rooms, but the doors have always been shut. It is big, though, make no mistake about that! We can keep looking around as well until we make a final decision. What about spending some time at the house with Carol this weekend?

'Yes, that' a good idea. We can work out if it will suit us as a family,' said Dave.

'Yeah! That's what Carol said as well'. They both then got a drink and put their feet up to watch a TV programme they were both interested in.

Sam phoned Carol and they arranged for the whole family to visit the following Saturday.

I'll do lunch', said Carol.

'Too much. We'll come for coffee and cake later.'

Chapter 26

The day came for them to go to Carol's. Dave found Alfie kneeling on a chair up to his elbows in the kitchen sink, soap suds everywhere!

'What are you doing?'

'Washing my football. It's dirty. I can't take it to Carol's like this.'

Dave smiled. 'Next time Alfie, you wash it in the garden.

'Mum's coming. Quick! Pull the plug out'. Alfie let the water out and ran into the garden with his football. Sam saw him standing on tiptoe trying to see through the kitchen window, as Dave washed down the kitchen sink. Sam went up to him.

'You are a good Dad' she said, without really knowing what was going on.

Carol stood at her front door greeting them as they all tumbled into her house. Alfie threw his arms around her waist making her blush and look embarrassed when Dave had to weave his way around them. Sam was next in with Grace in her arms.

They greeted each other Carol saying. 'No car seat for Grace to sit in?'

'Dave will have to get the travel cot out of the boot; it

serves as a play pen.' Looking confused Carol moved away from the door with Alfie still hanging onto her waist.

'Let Carol move Alfie' Sam shouted. He moved away but went back and took her hand.

'You are adorable' she said, as he continued holding her hand. Dave brought in the travel cot and set it up as Carol asked Alfie.

'Can I give Grace a cuddle now?'

'No!' he said, still holding her hand but then quickly let go of her hand, laughing.

Carol picked Grace up, looked her in the face and said. 'Hello! Beautiful'. Grace gurgled. Carol looked at Sam saying. 'Gosh!' She's getting heavier' while quickly putting her back down. They were all finally in and settled. Carol had bought the latest DVD for the children. She asked Sam if they could watch it and made coffee, then they began to talk about the house. Sam asked if the three of them could look around first, especially as Alfie seemed engrossed in the DVD. Dave called. 'Alfie!' He glanced up. Will you watch Grace while Carol takes us upstairs?'

'Ok Dad' he said, with one eye still on the TV.

There were certainly many rooms, all of different sizes, they could easily change it into a five-bedroom home with still rooms left to use.

'Wow! We could really spread out in this house' said Sam, sounding excited at the discovery.

'They came down to find both children as happy as Larks! Alfie chuckling at the TV and Grace making strange noises which they assumed was her laughing, too. There was coffee and cake and Alfie was asked to sit on the floor as Sam placed a plastic sheet in front of him to catch the crumbs. Carol said not to worry about any mess, but Sam said that its ok that's how they do things at home or else Alfie has to sit at the dining table. Grace's cake was slowly fed to her on her tongue by Sam. Carol laughed saying Grace's expressions were really cute as she tried to swallow and lick her lips all at once. They talked about the house. Carol invited them to try living there anytime. She could always stay in the flat, but she was very reluctant to mention money. Finally, Dave said. 'Sam told me you had the house valuated, what was it valued at?'

Carol looked at Sam.

'Carol injected Sam. We are going to buy this house if we decide upon it, so please let's just talk openly.' Carol told them the figure. Dave took out his notes from his pocket and placed them on the table. 'That is slightly less than the other houses in this area are listed at.' He pointed to the figures. Sam looked across to check on the children. 'So said Dave. We've an idea of what our house might be worth, so we'll need to make additional Mortgage arrangements.

'No! please don't take on another, or extend your present mortgage said Carol. I would suggest that you complete your present payments and only then start buying for my house. In the meantime, you can move in when-ever you like. It's like I said. I don't need the money and in any case I'm sure you'll need to spend a lot on it. The house is all mine, I have no one to account for what I do, so please, buy it at the figure it was valued at and when you are ready to start paying for it, it will be with no interest of-course'. She laughed, embarrassed.

The DVD had just ended. 'You stay and decide,' said Carol. 'I'll take the children into the garden'. Carol headed for the garden as Alfie ran after her, football in hand. Sam picked Grace up as Dave folded the carry cot in half and carried it outside, with toys still in it. He set Grace up again. Sam and Dave chatted as Alfie and Carol kicked the football around. They played within Grace's sight and she giggled excitedly. As Sam and Dave headed towards them in the garden, Carol watched. They seemed happy with their decision. She hoped that is was the same as hers. Sam picked Grace up and they walked around the grounds. The garden wrapped itself beautifully around the house. Dave remarked that it was a safe and secure garden for the children. 'That needs work too said Carol. Everything needs redoing'. She sounded upset, as if she was leaving a mess behind for them to deal with. Alfie happily ran and bounced around the garden; it was a big adventure for him due to its vastness.

'Do you like it here?' asked Sam as he ran back to them.

'Yeah! I could have a goal post there', he pointed.

'I thought you didn't like football', Dave said.

'Not to be in a team Dad, just to play'.

'Oh! I see' said Dave, knowing perfectly well what Alfie meant. By now Grace was getting heavy so Sam handed her over to Dave. Alfie ran on ahead. 'I could have a swing there and a tree house there. Shall we build Carol a tree house Dad?' he asked. They all laughed. They loved his innocence. Before leaving the house, Sam and Dave told Carol that thanks to her, they would not extend or take out another mortgage but while continuing to pay their present mortgage they will also pay her a monthly amount. Dave quoted her a figure.

'That's fine' she said simply. Whatever suits you. They asked if they could go upstairs again. 'It's practically yours, do what you like', Carol smiled at their happy faces. This time Alfie and Grace went with them, Alfie being allowed to have a good look around. He wondered from room to room whirling around in the space available sometimes with arms stretched out sideways, sometimes with them by his side. He even managed to be an aeroplane in one of the larger bedrooms. Dave causally asked Alfie what he thought about the house and garden and which would be his favourite bedroom. He could see the clogs in Alfie's mind beginning to turn. He pointed to a particular bedroom door. 'I like this one. Are we going to live with you, Carol?'

'No' said Dave, but mum and I are thinking of buying Carol's house, we need much more room now.'

'Where will Carol live?'

'In Tanya's flat, it is hers now'. Alfie thought for a while.

'There is plenty of room for Carol to live with us.'

'We'll soon fill these rooms up' laughed Sam trying to take Alfie's mind away from Carol.

With more coffee and cake awaiting them Carol asked. 'Do you like the house Alfie?'

'Yes! But I don't want you to move too far away.' She smiled as she went up to him saying. 'You are always here, placing her hand on Alfie's heart. For once he looked embarrassed and did not know what to say or do.

They chatted in general until Sam finally said; 'this little one needs a change.'

'We can go upstairs', said Carol. Dave realized that Carol probably wanted to spend some girl time with Sam. He glanced at the TV while hearing them chatting and laughing as Grace gurgled alongside them.

'They are happy,' said Alfie.

'They are son', said Dave just as they returned downstairs.

'We'll get going on the sale as soon as you like,' said Carol. I'll contact my solicitor'.

'So will we' grinned Dave.

The James house was soon put on the market as Carol began moving into Tanya's flat. The two women hardly had time to meet up, but both kept each other abreast of what was happening in their lives. Carol said she liked living next door to Queenie. 'She keeps me supplied with food and drink while I work on the flat. Giggling, she continued, we have lovely tea breaks with Queenie's tinkling teacups always on hand.'

Although Carol's tone seemed upbeat Sam could detect a touch of sadness in her voice. How strange must Carol feel she wondered, moving from a house she'd shared with a loving husband into her sister's flat, both parties being deceased now, a shiver went down her spine thinking about the strange fate of Carol's life.

Some structures of Carol's house needed improvement and so builders were around in force. Dave took Alfie to see the building trade in action, but secretly also to check that work was progressing at a reasonable pace. This time gap gave Sam and the family some light relief and fun as they went around looking for suitable wallpaper and paint for various rooms. Alfie was excited at being allowed to choose how he wanted his bedroom decorated and chose wallpaper with multi coloured building blocks, yes! Lego bricks of course! Sam insisted that only one wall was done in this wallpaper as the colours were quite overpowering, so surrounding walls were painted in a calm, cool, blue. Time rushed forward and as the builders moved out Sam and family moved in.

They had a buyer for their house and a completion and moving date was decided for a few months ahead. It was a frantic time indeed, but eventually they were settled in and life took on its own forms and routines. It was only then that they realized how much Grace had grown and matured, with the space they now had she was already walking a few steps and continued to show her strength and determination and soon walked firmly. Very rarely did she fall over. Her words and speech were also clearer than many children of her age.

The house was finally completed to their liking and Sam suggested that they have a housewarming party. As well as Sam's usual friends they also invited Dave's work mates and their families and his pub mates of many years. There were also various aged children around and the big secluded garden was wonderful, as they could heard having lots of fun outdoors. Grace weaved herself in and out of people in complete confidence, never getting knocked over, or falling down as Sam stood on tender hooks watching her, wanting to help, yet feeling useless. Sam had to make do with deep breaths to calm her at what she was witnessing. Grace was special, wasn't Sam being told that practically from the day she was born.

In quiet moments she mulled those words over and over in her mind. Grace was definitely showing herself to be special and found the other children almost by instinct and joined them, each group making her as welcome as the next. She helped herself to finger food and cold drinks spilling much less than some of the older children. Watching her through all of this Sam sighed as she found Carol suddenly standing beside her.

'How often have I felt that Grace has been here before, just look at her!'

'Well! Who knows? said Carol. There are so many theories on past lives; I don't even know what I believe anymore. Do you believe?'

'No! I don't said Sam. I thought I'd do better as my mind is constantly expanding with my psychic circle, books and classes, but the more validation I receive the more my thoughts go off in frenzy. It doesn't help when both Alfie and Grace show or tell me something, for although I have to believe, as it's just happed before me, this still throws up more questions than answers.' Dave joined Sam and Carol, but they were soon interrupted by guests wanting to say goodbye and thank their hosts.

Alfie and Grace were put to bed by Sam and Carol while Dave and Queenie cleared up downstairs. Sam took the opportunity to ask Carol how she felt about being back in her old house and also in Tanya's flat.

'Pretty strange to be honest', she said, in both cases, but I'm glad that all of you seem so happy here.'

'We are. Grace only came to the fore with her walking since we moved here. We're sure it's partly due to the additional space. Alfie is happy too but doesn't say much. He's a big boy now you know', she laughed. The women hugged their usual goodbye as Queenie and Carol left. Sam and Dave couldn't wait to get to bed themselves, they were exhausted. They kissed. Dave remarking what a good time everyone seemed to have. 'Our daughter is amazing and did you see the way she walked about?'

'Yes! She nearly gave me a heart attack each time I saw her.' They held hands as they fell asleep.

The following morning Sam woke with a start having heard one of the children moving around, she was about to get out of bed to check on them when Grace walked in.

'Mummy, Daddy' she announced in complete sentences. Didn't we have a lovely party?'

It was Dave's turn to wake up in shock. 'What did you say Darling?' Grace repeated the whole sentence as perfectly as the first time. That important moment was quickly lost as Alfie ran into the room and jumped all over Dave as their play fighting began. Grace lay on Sam having a cuddle. Sam was too much in shock to say anything. The family took their time and had a slow leisurely day. Finally, Sam quietly asked Grace. 'How did you learn to say all those words this morning?'

'I know how to talk Mummy and to walk, I just know.' She certainly did and from then on, she was a toddler with a knowing and knowledge way beyond her years.

Alfie was thrilled to hear Grace speak, whereas Sam thought that he may be jealous of her abilities, instead he said. 'Of course, Grace can talk, she's being talking to me since before she was even born, now we can talk out loud or in our minds.' Sam and Dave stared at each other; Sam opened mouthed. The children rushed off to play as if everything is as it should be.

Grace seemed to grow and develop everyday which led Sam to start thinking about her attending a local nursery. She had been teaching Grace her alphabets', numbers, colours and nursery rhymes, Grace whizzed through the lot. Alfie was doing great at school as well; they were surprising her with their intellect.

'Young they may be' Sam said to Dave, but they are bright and we must not let that slip away.' Dave agreed and soon their Saturday evenings consisted of board games of a learning nature. Colours, shapes and numbers were included in their games, then, when something else suddenly started to take place. Alfie and Grace were able to read the playing cards although they were placed face down on the table and they thought it was part of the game as Sam too, surprised herself by also being capable of reading the cards, but she was not as accurate as her children. Being able to read was fun until Dave freaked out. He shouted at them saying that they were all cheats and he didn't want cheats in his house, his aggression shocked Sam and had both children in tears.

He then walked off in a huff leaving Sam to calm the children down.

'Dad is worrying about us again' she said cuddling both children, while taking Grace upstairs to get her ready for bed.

'You get yourself ready too Alfie, and would you read to Grace?'

'Yes read' said Grace jumping up and down. Sam was relieved that the children had calmed down quickly as she returned downstairs. She gave the children time to relax and when she returned to check on them, she found Grace fast asleep with Alfie asleep beside her. She smiled happily at the sight but didn't want this to become a habit, so shook Alfie gently to wake him up and led him into his own bedroom and tucked him in. She kissed him good night and thanked him for reading to Grace. He hadn't forgotten. 'Is Dad still angry with us?'

'Don't worry love, I'll sort it out'. She wondered how often she'd have to keep sorting Dad out. She thought he was already sorted. She thought that he now understood and accepted their psychic abilities. She went into their bedroom expecting to see Dave. He wasn't there. She didn't know which spare bedroom he was in.

The next morning began with its usual school routine but there was no sign of Dave. Sam had already strapped Grace into the car. She was walking out the door when Dave shouted 'Wait!' Alfie turned as Dave walked over to him 'Bye son' he said, ruffling his hair.

'Bye dad,' said Alfie. Sam only smiled as they left.

The drive to school was noneventful and quiet and once they arrived Alfie went off to play with Tom. Sam looked at Grace in her rear-view mirror. 'Alright, love?' she asked. Grace smiled back; her angelic look still showing although her features had matured. When they got home, Sam told Grace to go off and play. She put the kettle on not knowing where Dave was.

He came out of his office upon hearing the kettle click off.

'Sorry' he said as he went over and kissed her. They heard a gentle voice say.

'Me too Daddy, kiss.' Both of them melted with pride and joy as Dave picked Grace up and kissed her. She giggled with glee. They made Grace a drink and all sat quietly just enjoying being near each other. Grace finally wriggled off Dave's lap and went back to her toys. Sam and Dave talked. Dave said how sorry he was about his behaviour the previous night and that he behaves like a mad man at times.

'We need to work out how to cope with our psychic abilities for all our sakes,' said Sam. Dave said that he had a plan. He would go over it when Alfie was back from school. Sam was curious but left it at that. Their day progressed normally.

It was when Alfie was doing his homework that Dave's plan was put into action so he asked Alfie to do some sums which he had set for him, watching intently as Alfie worked on them. When he had finished Dave gave Alfie much praise for they were all correct. He said that he was pleased that Alfie had worked out all the answers, on his fingers when necessary, for this proved to him that he wasn't reading the answers from Dave's mind. Sam took over the conversation as Grace stood beside her.

'What I want both of you to do is to promise Dad and me that you will never be horrible or bully other children if you know something about them, and that you will never tell others of your ability. This will only give them the opportunity to tease you or ask you for more information. If you have any problems, come home and talk to us first.

'But, said Alfie. Dad doesn't understand.' Sam was about to speak. Dave touched her knee to stop her.

'I might not ever understand Alfie', but I will always listen and I promise I will not shout at any of you about this again. I'm sorry that I called you cheats last night it was horrible of me to that.'

'Alfie, said Sam. It is better if you keep quiet rather than get into trouble. Remember the story of Tom and his Grandad, we got away with that, but we don't want something like that to happen again. I know you have learnt many good tips from the book Queenie gave you, always remember to keep other people's feelings in mind and you will be fine'. Sam noticed Grace was still standing by her side and was sure that she had taken in the whole conversation. To lighten the load Dave said. 'Mum's already started cooking, but how about we go out for a quick ice-cream later?'

'Thanks dad' said Alfie as Grace went over and gave him a kiss. Sam smiled.

'She has you around her little finger' she whispered in Dave's ear.

'Like mother, like daughter', he whispered back.

'It's rude to whisper' laughed Alfie as he ran across the room.

Chapter 27

The days, months and years flew by as Sam and her family continued with their lives. Grace began nursery and then progressed into their main feed school. The two children being at different schools turned out fine, although it meant that both Dave and Sam had to drive each child to school as they now started at the same time.

Dave was happy with his extra space and his business grew, so all in all life was good and settled. Sam still attended the Spiritual Church but other than that she's stopped sitting in circle and led a normal, pretty quiet life. The children had no more psychic experiences either and were happy with their school, and friends, which was why Sam was startled when she realized that Grace was a Healer. Her healing ability came about when Sam fell down the stairs. She put it down to just an accident as she was carrying a full basket of laundry and trying to negotiate the stairs at the same time, as she fell, she banged her right elbow against the wall, letting out a squeal, she sat on the stair, stunned. Grace went over to her and gently rubbed her elbow saying. 'It's all right mum.' The pain immediately began to dissipate and was soon gone. Dave noticed that Sam's scowl, brought on by pain also disappeared as he stood at the bottom of the stairs, watching

'How did you do that, Darling?

'I don't know mum, but I have been doing it for a long time.'

Sam walked into the living room with Dave and sat in a comfy chair.

'Will you tell us more?' asked Sam. Dave made Grace a soft drink and switched on the kettle for the pair of them.

'At nursey' said Grace a little boy fell and hurt his knee. He was crying and upset saying that it hurt. The teacher was talking to him as I went over and rubbed his knee. He stopped crying and said that he was all better. He ran off to play.'

'What did the teacher say?' asked Dave.

'She said something about me having magic in my hands. I didn't understand.'

'You could do this at three years old? Grace nodded.

'Can I go and play?

'Of course, said Sam.'

Grace smiled at them. Dave made tea and they sat and drank it in shock.

Alfie appeared and asked Dave to sit with him, his homework was getting more varied and harder and as he moved further up the school. Sam heard Grace practicing her reading and went to join her. She was so proud of both her children she only hoped that nothing would disrupt their education.

In bed Dave and Sam talked about Grace. Did she really

have the power to heal?' Sam suddenly remembered that when Grace had rubbed her elbow, she felt a surge of warmth. It seemed to penetrate right through her skin and flesh and arrive deep into her bone. That's better than seeing the dead!' said Dave. Sam didn't know if she should laugh or cry. His statement sounded so flippant.

Dave soon fell asleep, but Sam was wide awake, believing this was so special and significant it made her want to find out more. She got up and went into the kitchen, grabbed the laptop and sat at the dining table. It was then that she thought she saw a shadow, but she quickly put the thought aside. It wasn't just a thought, for a few moments later the figure of a woman manifested before her, she plainly showed himself. Here was her evidence. Not again! She thought. 'Allow your children to fly. No harm will come to anyone. They will be grounded although they can fly', her words were as clear as day.

'Who are you?' She asked quietly, so as not to wake anyone.

'An Angel' replied the voice, and then she was gone, leaving Sam with a feeling of peace and love, and a wondering of recognition of the Angel. Taking a deep breath Sam typed into the search engine. Is healing a psychic/spiritual possibility? There was her answer her explanation! Healing is the ability of being able to direct new energy into injured areas, this taking away any pain and discomfort. She also noted that the healer is known for his/her empathy. God, bless her, thought Sam, Grace has always been known for her very caring disposition.

The next morning Dave found Sam looking at her photograph albums. 'What are you up to?' he asked.

'Remembering. My parents and family died so long ago I have to try really hard in order to remember what everyone was like.'

Dave sat down beside her. 'No work?' she asked.'

'Plenty, it's just that you looked so sad.'

'I'm alright,' said Sam. She couldn't tell Dave that what she was really looking for was someone who resembled the Angel who had appeared to her as an ordinary woman.'

'Cup of tea, help?' He asked. She nodded. Dave disappeared. He returned a few minutes later and handed her the tea, he kissed her on her forehead and returned to his office.

Sam was glad that she had her photographs in order with names and dates on the back as a double reference, at first, she found nothing, flipping through them again something caught her eye, taking it out of the album she studied it further. She looked on the back and saw the name Jayne. Aunty Jayne was her mum's sister. Here, Jayne looked the spitting image of Grace. In the snap she was older than Grace, but there was no doubt of their likeness. Sam sat in deep thought as she sipped her tea, trying to remember any stories she might have heard from her mum about Jayne, but her mind was sadly a complete blank. Knowing that Dave was around she tried not to dwell on things too much, she would only get sad again. In her dwelling she remembered that there was a box with special papers and other items, she was sure that her mum's diary was amongst them. She always wanted to go through those papers but had never done so. When she found the box again while moving the thought reoccurred to her, now she had to look in there! Wanting to go through these treasures alone.

Dave was home so much now; would she ever get the chance she wondered. Luck was on her side. She heard Dave's mobile ring. A short while later he came over to tell her that his work partners had found a new restaurant so they wanted to meet there for lunch and he had agreed to join them.

Smiling, she said, 'That's fine love.' She didn't want to say too much, her emotions were swirling around inside and any outpour of them around Dave would not have helped.

When Dave left to meet his partners, she rushed into the spare bedroom and got out the box of papers and had a quick look at them. Nothing in particular registered with her. Later, before leaving to collect Grace from school, she hid the box at the back of her wardrobe on the top shelf. It reminded her of the time she had hid her psychic books away from Dave.

Sam had a long wait until the next morning before she had time and space to get back to the box of papers and her photograph albums again. She made herself some tea and sat at the dining table going through the albums more carefully this time, laying before her the photographs especially chosen. Mum and Dad looked perfect together she thought. I still blame myself at times. Of-course I know that it was never my fault, but the fact that they were on their way to meet me and take me out to dinner to celebrate my birthday still makes me feel guilty. They both died instantly, even before they got to me, as another car jumped a red light and ploughed into them. Her eyes filled with tears, this was why she wanted to be alone looking at more photographs of herself, playing in the park, her birthdays, and dad pushing her on the swings. She hadn't thought of these wonderful times for years. She must get the albums out for the children to look at. Sam looked at the photograph of her mum and couldn't see any resemblance between the two of them, nor did Grace look like her mum. Looking at the image of Aunty Jayne; there it was again, those remarkable features which perfectly matched those of Grace. She sighed as she tried to swallow a lump forming in her throat and ended up almost choking herself instead. She coughed and coughed and got up to get herself a glass of water

feeling grateful that no one else was around. She scanned the photograph of the young Aunty Jayne and also one of Grace and placed them side by side.

'My Goodness! They looked more like sisters than Mum and Aunty Jayne did. Gasping, she touched Aunty Jayne's photograph almost unconsciously, she felt a slight heat arising, making her hand feel warm, and then it was gone. Energy! She thought that's what I learnt. Many items and objects hold the owner's energy for many years. Aunty Jayne has just proved that.

'Thank you' she said to the air. You are welcome, said a distant voice in her head. The tears poured this time, as confused feelings continued to engulf her. Sam wanted to remember, but that made her sad, now, she was wondering what to do with herself when her mobile rang.

'Hello! Carol, how are you?'

'Can I come over if you're not busy?'

'Sure' said Sam.

She cleared away her albums and tided around a bit before Carol arrived. She had a guest with her.

'Ben!' said Sam. Some-what surprised.

'Hello! 'said Ben, shaking her hand.

'Come in, come in. I'll put the kettle on.

She thought that Carol's voice sounded high pitched and giddy in the recent few short moments in which she had spoken to her, now again she spoke in that same voice.

'Ben and I are going to live together' she said excitedly.

'I would rather get married'. Ben chimed in.

'We'll see,' said Carol.

Sam was stunned. 'Either way Congratulations! She said.

'Well! said Ben. Look at this'. He took Carol's hand and held it out. It was a gold band engagement ring, with a blue sapphire stone surrounded by small diamonds.

'Wow! said Sam. That's like Princess Diana's.'

'Not really' blushed Ben. But pretty don't you think? Just like my fiancé'.

'You two are blowing my mind! It's all too much for me to take in' said Sam. Ben and Carol laughed, happy to be sharing their good news.

'I'm moving into Ben's house' volunteered Carol. It's easier all round as Noah stays most weekends and we don't want to mess up his routine by buying another place and moving away.

'Noah?' questioned Sam.

'My son', said Ben. Remember, he was at the skating rink?' Sam smiled.

'I know our getting engaged may seem very rushed, but I'm no spring chicken,' laughed Carol.

Ben cuddled her. 'You're gorgeous', he said. They sat and drank a small glass of wine, just to celebrate the good news. Sam was disappointed that Carol hadn't told her of their intentions on her own, but she knew that everyone was busy and they hadn't been keeping in touch as often as they used to.

They continued chatting.

'Queenie is going to miss me, I think, but I'll see what I will do about the flat at a later date.

'Sam listened, not believing what she was hearing. The time had gone so quickly that she could still remember Carol shrugging her shoulders dismissing the idea of her being with Ben.

'I know what, Carol suddenly said. Let's have a girly night, if it's ok with Dave. Where is he by the way?'

'Out with his business partners', said Sam.

'Anyway, continued Carol. Why don't you stay at my flat, then we can get together with Queenie as well. Can Dave manage with both children for one night, at least?' Sam was beginning to feel insulted. Carol didn't bother to tell her about her and Ben, she could have rung, now, she expects Dave to be home with the kids while she stays out all night. Why are you looking so angry?' Carol asked Sam.

'Nothing. Thoughts running away with me, sorry.' She was happy for Carol; just sometimes she guessed others put

themselves first without realizing it. That's what she felt that
Carol at done over time and is still doing it even more now.

Carol and Ben continued to sit happily on Sam' couch.
They didn't seem in any hurry to leave, so Sam put the kettle
on. She checked the fridge.

'Want some lunch?' she shouted from the kitchen. 'Nothing fancy. Cheese and ham, ok?' She walked back into the
living room. They were both sitting, staring at Carol's ring,
oblivious of everything else, so she returned to the kitchen.
They must have snapped out of it, for she found Carol standing next to her as she buttered the bread.

'For us?' Carol asked. She looked so happy that Sam went
over and hugged her.

'You really are in love.' Carol blushed as the kettle clicked
off and she began making tea for everyone. They called
Ben over and ate lunch together. When Ben excused himself,
Carol said. 'You will come and stay over, won't you? I do
want to talk to you alone. It's just been such a crazy time.'
'I'll come and see you and I'd love to see Queenie, but I won't
stay over. It's not fair to Dave.' Carol smiled and nodded in
agreement. Ben was on his way back to the table when Dave
walked in the back door.

'I know you!' said Dave.

'Ben'. They shook hands.

'Show Dave', said Sam. Carol went over and pecked Dave
on the cheek, showing him her sparkling engagement ring.
Ben moved in alongside her.

'Congratulations!' said Dave. 'When did all this happen?'

'I'll fill you in love,' said Sam, seeing that both Carol and

Ben were beginning to look uncomfortable. Carol said that she would be in touch with Sam as they hugged each other goodbye.

Sam was surprised to hear from Carol within only a few days.

'Hello! Time for a coffee? Can you come here, you can see Queenie too, come for lunch?'

Sam went to Carol's. They had lunch at Queenie's, once again alongside her tinkling teacups, and enjoyed time spent together. Carol explained to Sam that life just seemed to happen, rushing her and Ben along in their relationship.

'I remember what I told you about not wanting to get involved with Ben, but we just hit it off from the start and it progressed from there.'

'I know,' said Sam. I can see how happy and in love you are. How are you with his son?'

'I was worried, and still am in some ways, but he does seem to like me a lot.'

'See! I've always told you that you are good with children.'

'Yes. I am very careful though. I've not yet spent a weekend at Ben's as Noah is always with him, so I stay at my flat. Ben thinks that it's time I did stay with them but'... She looked at Sam. 'I'm not sure'.

'What? Why?' asked Sam.

'I'm scared'.

'What off?' Carol looked not just scared but terrified. Sam could see it in her eyes.

'I don't know. Having to be well, a step mum I guess.'

'You will be, but I assure you that you will be great.' Carol began to shake. Sam knew that she was really scared of the prospect.

'Oh! Carol. I don't understand why you feel this way. Look how great you are with my two. Carol was at the point of tears.

'You daft thing!' said Sam. You will be wonderful.' Sam offered her tissues, as by now Carol was crying again. You're just emotional. It will all be good. Have you spoken to Ben about it?'

'He says I'll be fine. I'm worrying too much.'

'I told you'.

'As I said we do get on great' said Carol again, but I don't feel connected to Noah as I do to your Alfie and Grace.'

'It takes time, Carol. You've known us for ages. Spend as much time, including weekends, she winked at Carol, and you will get to know each other far better. Just as friendships grow, so will your relationship with Noah. What does Ben's ex-wife think?' Asked Sam.

'According to Ben she doesn't care, she just likes her weekends to herself.'

'Have you spoken to her?'

'No. Never met her.'

'Did you not see her at the ice rink?'

'No. Did you?' Asked Carol.

'Yes'. What does she look like? Is she pretty?'

Sam laughed. 'You are the pretty one Carol she said. I only saw her from the back anyway. Ben took Noah's bag from her. She was watching Noah all the time. How about this? asked Sam. Why don't the three of you come and have a

Sunday with us. You can get to know Noah and he can spend time with Alfie. How old is he?'

'Twelve.'

'That should work out. Alfie is ten. They should get along.'

Is Alfie ten? That means that Grace is seven years old.'

'Yes!' Said Sam laughing at the shocked expression on Carol's face. Sam knew that Carol was getting into a state about her life with Ben. 'Call me, said Sam. Anytime you want to talk.' Carol promised that she would.

Sam talked to Dave about Carol's worries and uncertainties.

'It's just nerves, love. She can't imagine what her future will be like.'

Chapter 28

Everyone's life seemed to carry on, although Sam did notice that Alfie was less outgoing and less outspoken then he used to be.

'You're very quiet these days. Is everything alright?'

'Yes mum.' Was all she got out of him. Tom still stayed over-night sometimes and Alfie stayed at his house. Sam decided that it was time to have a coffee with Kate. They made arrangements, Kate asking Sam if they could meet at her home, this giving them more time together before Kate had to rush back to school for her dinner time job. They talked and laughed and although Sam didn't want to ask any outright questions, she stirred the conversation onto the boys', starting by talking causally about how Alfie and Tom were growing up and how they had remained friends after all this time, especially given their unfriendly start, ending by saying. 'Is Alfie still well behaved? Well-mannered and so on?'

'Of course, said Kate sounding surprised at the question Why?'

'He's just gone a bit into himself at home. Not as... how shall I put it... Bright and breezy as he used to be.'

'I don't find him any different, honestly Sam', said Kate.

'Worrying about nothing. Just being a mum. You know how it is.'

'Yes, I do,' said Kate. Sam left Kate's feeling as if she'd achieved nothing and still her intuition told her that something was a bit off, un-settled, perhaps. Sam felt so worried about Alfie that she even asked Dave to keep an eye on him.

'You and Carol he said. Worriers!'

Sam smiled but said, 'Remember, keep an eye on Alfie for me.'

Carol phoned to say that her, Ben and Noah would like to come over that Sunday if they were free but would stop for only a few hours. We'll see you at four o'clock.

'That's great' said Sam thinking that the conversation was over.

'Sam?'

'Yes'.

'Can I stay over with all of you for the night?'

'Why?' Surely you can stay at Ben's. Won't Noah go back to his mother's that night?

'It's ok if I can't,' said Carol. Sounding embarrassed.

'You can stay anytime Carol. I didn't mean it like that'

'Can I come over earlier?'

'Come for Sunday lunch,' said Sam.

'I'll like that. I'll tell Ben to meet us at four o'clock. I'll give him your address.'

'Whatever you like Carol, said Sam. See you Sunday'. Sam came away from the house phone shaking her head and looking puzzled.

'What's up? asked Dave. You look confused'. Sam told him about Carol's phone call.

'Sounds to me like Carol is very unsure of herself. If she has all these doubts and fears let's hope she doesn't rush into marriage.' Dave walked away, leaving Sam with much to think about.

Carol turned up on the Sunday as happy as ever. Sam didn't tell the children that she was coming over. They both looked surprised when the doorbell rang. Grace ran to the window. It's Carol's car' she shouted excitedly', as Alfie ran past his mum and opened the door. As soon as Carol stepped in, he threw his arms around her waist as usual.

'Gosh!' she said. You've grown so much'. Sam walked over and gently prised him off her. The two women hugged hello! When Sam moved away Grace was standing behind her. Carol bent at the knees and said 'Hello! Beautiful. Grace hugged her neck. Got to stand up again Darling' she said as Sam helped her straighten up. They all laughed. Dave, having heard Carol arrive had put the kettle on. He soon handed each of them a cup of tea as he welcomed Carol. Both children went into the garden. Dave followed them mug of tea in hand.

The women chatted as usual catching up on their daily lives. Sam was determent not to ask Carol too much about Ben, although she longed to. They went into the garden.

'You've done wonders with the garden' she said. Flowers, everything nice and neat'.

'Dave too, said Sam, he does a lot of the heavier work, but we do in joy it.', then they walked around seeing Alfie's goal and the tree house. Alfie ran over and took Carol's hand. Grace hung out of the tree house door and between them they got her into it. Alfie also climbed in and when Sam called out, they all looked down as Sam quickly took a lovely photograph of all three on her mobile.

Carol was so relaxed and happy, it filled Sam with pride and joy to think that her family could make someone else feel so wanted and loved. Dave and Sam were busy with the vegetables when the three came back in.

'Can I borrow your children?' asked Carol. Dave and Sam said together.

'What?'

'Can I take them to the toy shop?' Alfie's and Grace's eyes got as big as saucers.

'Please! I haven't seen them in ages'.

'OK.' said Sam, but they don't need anything!' The children jumped in joy, as Dave called them over to him and reminded them of curtesy and manners. They all went off laughing and talking. Sam and Dave were glad to see Carol enjoying herself. Recently she seemed to be strangely happy and stressed out at the same time, especially whenever Ben came into the conversation. Sam couldn't wait to see him and his son together.

Needless to say, Carol and the children returned with lots of toys, books, colouring pencils and much more. She had bought Grace her first Lego set. A pink and white, girly one! Carol sat on the floor and went through all their new gifts with them, laughing, talking and sharing. She tickled and cuddled them; they were all so happy together. Alfie seemed to be his cheeky out going self again. They were all so good for each other. Eventually they sat down for Sunday lunch when Sam asked, 'Were Alfie and Grace polite and good for you while out Carol?'

'As always' said Carol. The children looked up and grinned at their parents with mouths full of food.

'How is school? Carol asked Alfie. Is, Tom, is it? Still your best friend?'

'Yes', said Alfie, as he told Carol about an incident at school with him and Tom playing football. It was quite a conversation from Alfie, something he'd not being doing with them of late. She asked Grace the same question.

'I like school' she said. I like it best when I can help people.

'How do you mean, beautiful? Grace looked at her parents.

'I can make other children all better if they get hurt, she said, and it makes me feel good.'

'What do your teachers say?' asked Carol.

'They say I have magic fingers or now, they sometimes say magic hands, then they go off and start talking together.'

'Do you know what they say?'

'Sometimes, I've heard them say that I must be special. Sometimes they say I am strange. I don't care. I do it because I can and know that I am meant to'. It was Carol's turn to look at Sam and Dave, Sam understood her look.

'Do you know what you are really? Asked Carol.

'Yes! I am a healer, I heal people'. Dave choked on his food.

'That is special indeed, beautiful said Carol. You are very brave as well not to allow people to stop you from doing your healing, although they may laugh or tease you.' Grace shrugged her shoulders and asked if she could have more chicken.

Sam and Dave were once again amazed how Grace had opened up to Carol. She'd never spoken so much about her ability before. Carol thanked Sam for the meal.

'I feel full up' she said.

'Go and have a comfy seat,' said Sam.

'Let me help clear up.'

Dave said, 'the children love you, go and sit with them, you are like their Aunty.' Carol went into the living room.

'Can we watch the DVD now? Asked Alfie.

'What DVD is that? Shouted Sam.

'Carol just bought it for us' said Grace.

'Oh! said Sam. OK'. Alfie put on the DVD.' Soon they could be heard laughing, as all three enjoyed themselves. Sam and Dave joined them, taking in a cup of tea for Carol. Looking at them again a while later Sam and Dave laughed. In spite of the TV being on loud all three had fallen asleep. Dave left the TV on but turned the volume down, as him and Sam split the newspaper and sat reading until the doorbell rang and Dave went to answer it.

Upon opening the door Dave held out his hand and expected Ben to offer his in return. He didn't, so Dave stepped aside and waved him and his son in.

Ben walked over and saw Carol asleep. Ignoring Sam who was setting nearby, he shouted.

'Carol!' She woke up startled. Her jerk also waking up Alfie and Grace as each had their head resting on one of her shoulders. That's nice and cosy' he said. He practically pulled Carol out of her seat.

'Sorry!' she mumbled still in a daze; I didn't mean to fall asleep.'

'Obviously not' said Ben, his voice becoming more sarcastic at every word he spoke.

'Sit down please' said Sam as she pointed to the couch. To everyone's surprise Carol got up and went to put the kettle on. Ben and Noah sat down with a gap between them leaving a place for Carol, Sam presumed. Upon her return Carol stood before them.

'Sit! It sounded like an order from Ben. It was plain to see that Carol was taken aback. What's wrong? You can't sit between us but you can sit between those two?' Father and son glared at Alfie and Grace. The two boys continued glaring at each other.

'How old are you?' asked Sam hoping to ease the tension. It didn't work, for Noah yelled back 'What's it to you?'

'Just trying to make conversation,' said Sam.

'Well! Don't bl***y bother' yelled Noah. Alfie stood up.

'Don't swear in front of my mum, sister and Carol he shouted. That's not nice at all!'

'That's not nice at all' repeated Noah in a sing song teasing voice. You sound like a girl.'

'I am not! Shouted Alfie stretching to his full height.

'You are certainly not a man! You are just a little boy. See! Shouted Noah while walking over to Alfie and pushing him hard in the chest. Alfie fell onto the comfy chair behind him. He stood up again. Noah pushed him again. Dave shouted.

'Stop that! I will not have a bully in my home!' Alfie's face looked like thunder. His voice was strong, bass very manly.

'It's alright Dad, he said. I can handle this.' He stood up again and as anticipated Noah tried to push him backwards again, but this time to no avail. Alfie had prepared himself. He now stood with feet firmly planted to the floor. Noah tried again. No effect this time either. Noah tried to get nearer Alfie, but as soon as he moved, he tripped over his own feet falling heavily to the floor.

'I bet that hurt. Look! Your nose is beginning to bleed. Not like me. I fell into a soft chair' Alfie sniggered. He loved getting his own back on Noah. Sam, Carol and even Grace seemed to know what and how Alfie had achieved the upper hand. It was by auto suggestion. Alfie had primed himself to be brave and strong and so his subconscious mind adapted to his ideas and thoughts allowing him to bring them to his aid. Ben helped Noah up from the floor and they headed to the front door in a fury.

'Come on Carol!' Ben demanded once again. All the family willed her not to go. Carol stood firm and said, 'I'll ring you tomorrow.' Everyone took a deep breath and let out a sigh of relief.

'I'm sorry about all that carry on said Carol. Ben usually treats me like a Queen, Noah too. He doesn't say much but he is gentle and kind'.

'I've met Ben, Carol. I know he can be different. May be he was jealous seen you so at home with all of us', said Sam, trying to account for Ben's bad behaviour. Carol looked at Alfie.

'Are you alright, love?'

'Yes. I'm glad you didn't go with them'.

'Me too' said Grace while taking Carol's hand.

'My Guardian Angles' said Carol as she cuddled them into her, and as she did so Grace touched Alfie's chest. He took a deep breath, and then said. 'Thanks Sis. It feels much better.' Grace smiled as everyone looked on.

Sam glanced at her watch. 'Time up! Teeth and bed please. School tomorrow.' They both looked at Carol. 'No chatting time, she said.

'But I'll come up and say quick goodnight'. They both beamed at Carol.

When Carol returned downstairs Sam asked her if she had brought any stay over bits with her.

'Yes, I'll get them from the car'. She picked up her handbag and got her car keys out.

'I'll help' said Dave following her. Carol opened her car boot as Dave took out her small case, she shut the boot electronically. Dave ushered her into the house. Sam was watching from the window as Dave looked around and up and down the street as he walked in behind Carol. Upon coming in Dave locked the front door, checked the French windows and back door. He wished them both good night saying he'll be in his office for a while. Sam wondered what Dave's cloak and dagger behaviour was all about, but didn't get a chance to ask him.

Carol took herself up to the spare room which she'd used before. She spread her toiletries around the bathroom. Sam had a glass of wine awaiting her upon her return downstairs.

The two chatted, but not about what had just transpired. Carol's mobile suddenly rung unexpectedly. Sam noticed it on the dining table and pointed to it. Carol answered it.

'Queenie. What's wrong? Are you alright?'

'I'll be right there.'

'What?' asked Sam. Carol looked upset.

'My flat has been broken into. Queenie has phoned the police. I need to go.'

'Let me go with you,' said Sam.

I'm fine' said Carol, but she wasn't. She was shaking.

'Wait! Just a minute, please' said Sam as she found Dave and told him quickly what had happened. 'Would you go with her?

'Of course,' said Dave. It took a bit of time to persuade Carol, but she finally agreed. She could have driven, having had only a sip of wine before the phone call, but Sam didn't want her going on her own. As Dave was walking towards the door Sam kissed him quickly on the lips and said. 'Please bring Queenie back too.'

'I will, if I can, love' he said.

'You are wonderful' she smiled. She took his hands and then let go of them as Dave continued on his way out with Carol behind him.

Dave drove, as each sat quietly, until Dave pulled into the parking space at Carol's flat. They headed to the front entrance and were shocked to see a policeman stationed there.

'Crime scene, madam he said. Afraid I can't let you in.'

'The crime is in my flat' said Carol producing her driving licence as I.D. having explained who she was.

'Sorry Madam' said the officer stepping aside. Carol climbed the few stairs, unsteadily. She was completely shocked at what she found. The front door was completely off its hinges and lying flat on the hallway floor, with police all over her flat. They were checking everything while taking photographs and fingerprints. She gasped at the sight.

'My flat, let me in' she said in a trembling voice. Dave wasn't doing much but was glad to be with her all the same. A female detective came over and introduced herself to Carol. 'Do you know if my friend Queenie is ok?

'Yes. One of our officers is interviewing her right now. I suggest we get this over with quickly. Would you have a look around, if you can, she half smiled. I know there are people everywhere. Please let us know if you notice anything missing.' Carol wandered through the flat almost in a daze, glancing at everything now strewn around, which were mostly clothes. Every drawer had been rummaged through and tipped out in all the rooms. Hanging garments were prised off their hangers and tossed aside. Carol just about held back the tears.

'Do you have any jewellery, expensive items, and important papers anywhere? Asked the detective This seemed to register with Carol. It pulled her out of her daze. She went to her hanging wardrobe and ran her hand along the top shelf. Luckily, the box was still there. Taking off the lid Carol glanced through the papers and lifted a section of the box away and noticing that the jewellery still there. The detective was beside her. 'Everything accounted for?' she asked.

'Looks like it. Just sentimental bits' said Carol. While she was talking Carol could see out the corner of her eye that Dave was talking to one of the policemen.

She found out later that they were discussing the measurements of the front door. Dave went over to Carol. 'We've got to make this flat safe, he said. Would it be ok for me to board it up for now? I'll get a new door and fix it up for you tomorrow.'

'Oh! Dave. I'm so sorry for all this trouble. You have your own family to worry about.'

'I'd better go to the hardware store before they shut' he said, go and stay with Queenie when everyone leaves here, won't you?' She looked at him with tears in her eyes. She could not believe the strange ways in which her life was going.

Dave bought a sheet of plywood wood, nails and a hammer with which to do the job and got on with it. Carol came out of Queenies and helped him sturdy the wood while he nailed it into the framework.

Queenie must have waited for him to stop banging. 'The kettle is on dears' she shouted to them. Over tea Queenie told Dave that she had told the police that it was Ben and she assumed his son, who broke into Carol's flat. Carol blushed. Dave was not sure why. He didn't know if it was out of embarrassment at choosing the wrong man, or the fact that Queenie saw fit to tell the police who exactly it was. Whichever, did not matter for Queenie and Carol seemed fine together.

Poor Dave was tired; he enjoyed his hot cup of tea, once again with Queenies tinkling teacups on hand. There was a big debate as to where the pair of them should stay. Queenie said that Carol could stay with her. In the end Dave announced.

'The pair of you won't want me to get into trouble with Sam, would you? I rung her while I was out and told her I'll bring both of you home.' They could not make up their minds if Dave was fibbing or not, but both agreed to go with him.

Chapter 29

Upon returning to Sam and Dave's house there was chicken and salad on the table. They were asked to help themselves but it was only Dave who tucked into everything.

'I'm sorry. I keep getting all of you involved in my life, my unpleasant life,' said Carol.

'Friends help each other, that's all we are doing' said Sam, as Queenie agreed.

'I don't want Alfie and Grace disrupted' Carol said, sighing.

'Being at the other end of the house I don't think they will realize that you are both here, but if you could stay there until we take them to school that will really help. If they see your car Carol, we'll make up some excuse for it being here.' Carol looked around sadly.

The morning went as planned and they got both children off to school with no questions asked. When Sam returned after dropping Grace off there was no sign of Dave, but Queenie and Carol were seated at the dining table. Dave's in his office,' said Carol. He's talking about fixing my door, but I need to go back and tidy and clean up anyway, as awful as it is. I can buy a new door on the way and get the shop workers to come and fit it.'

'Do both of you want to come back here and stay, while the front door is being sorted?'

'Carol can stay with me,' said Queenie.

'Do you think it is safe?' Asked Sam. Both of them nodded.

'I think they would have gone as far away as possible,' said Carol. The police said they would check Ben's house. I haven't heard back, but I guess he was not there. I don't even know where his son and ex-wife live or who Ben works for. You must think I'm really stupid.'

'It's alright' said Sam, giving Carol a tight hug. '

Please thank Dave again for everything and you too,' said Carol. Sam gave Queenie a goodbye peck on the cheek and there was another quick cuddle for Carol, as Sam felt so sorry for her.

Walking into the sitting room Dave said. 'I don't know about you but I feel shattered.'

'Thank you again love' Sam said. You were my superhero last night.'

'How about this superhero takes his super wife to bed?'

'Only if you wear your pants on the outside,' laughed Sam.

'Why not?' said Dave. Superman! I shall be! After all, we are on our own at last!'

Sam hadn't heard from Carol all day but knew she would receive a call from her. It was late when it came. The children were already in bed.

'Hello! Carol, are you ok?' asked Sam.

'Fine' she said. Better than I imagined I would be. Can you talk?'

'Yes. All quiet here. Dave is working. Children in bed. Me, with a glass of wine in my hand, fire away!'

'I was very negative about this flat Carol began. What, with the front door of its hinges. Police everywhere and the rest, who could blame me? But, I woke up in a very positive mood and so I've kept myself busy getting things in order. Thank Dave again for me. He was super!' Sam smiled to herself thinking about earlier when they joked about Dave being superman and what that had led to. Are you there? Asked Carol.

'Sorry! Mind just drifted. Will tell you about it sometime. Carry on'.

'Well, the man in the shop suggested I get a spy hole installed in my door so I got that done. The door is heavy and more solid so all in all I feel very safe. I tided and cleaned up again and have decided to modernise the place, especially the kitchen. I'd been thinking I should move out, that it was Tanya's flat, maybe it was jinxed. This morning, however, I am going to get me a new kitchen built. How's that for being positive?'

'Brilliant' said Sam.

'Yes. I need to be positive and keep busy so that's what I intend doing.

'Great! Any news from the police? Asked Sam.

'Oh! yes. They finally found Ben. Apparently, he apologized for himself and Noah saying they got jealous when they saw how happy and comfortable, I was with all of you.

They were in a rage about it and wanted to hurt and scare me. Wrecking my flat was their twisted revenge. Nothing has been stolen so they couldn't charge them with theft, but they were cautioned on the grounds of Domestic Disturbance. I could press charges, but I said no. I just want them out of my life, positive me again,' Carol laughed nervously.

'You sound like you are doing great. Keep it up! By the way, where is your engagement ring? I don't remember you wearing it on Sunday.'

'I totally forgot about it. I'm going to put you on speaker now.'

Sam heard a lot of shuffling noises. 'Yes, it's here. I wrapped it up in a tissue and put it in my handbag, it was never very practical to wear. I intended putting it on before they came over. You know the rest... she trailed off. I would like to return it, but don't want the contact, so it's just in my box here at the moment.'

'You sound really upbeat about your life again, that's really good.'

'The fact that I always had doubts says everything. You know how our intuition works Sam. I'm going to concentrate on myself and my little Guardian Angels how are they?'

'Little devils' said Sam pretending to be serious.

'I'll talk to you soon Sam'.

'If you need anything just let us know' said Sam. Carol said bye! And was gone. A quick exit thought Sam, but at lease she left on a positive note.

Dave was pleased when Sam told him about Carol's new, positive approach to her life.

'Leave her for a bit, won't you love? She needs time to continue working things out.'

Time passed as quickly as ever. Sam and Carol spoke but didn't meet up. Carol said she was busy and it was left at that. Queenie and Carol also kept in touch, but at the same time did not live in each other's pockets, they did things together but also respected each other's time and privacy.

Carol and Sam met totally by accident one evening at the Spiritualist Church. They sat and talked in Sam's car for a while but Sam found Carol to be a bit evasive. She wondered why. Within a few days she got her answer as Carol asked all of them over to her flat. 'I know it's a bit small but I'm sure we can manage, she said. I thought a Saturday afternoon would be nice and if the children get a bit fed-up, we could take them to the park.'

'I agreed' said Sam telling Dave about it. I think she wants us to see her new look flat.

'Fine, said Dave. He grinned. It's been too quiet around here.' Sam playfully punched him on the shoulder.

The children were very excited. They ran up the few stairs banging their feet and laughing.

'Quiet!' said Sam. There are other people living all around here.'

'What's all that noise?' smiled Carol coming out of the flat to greet them. Alfie put his arms around her waist as she walked backwards into the flat. The others followed as she hugged Grace and said. 'Hello! Beautiful'. The rest of the family did their usual greetings.

The women chatted as Carol showed them around. The

kitchen was adorned with all new units and sink. There was a new small desk and chair in the corner of the living room, surrounded by a new bookcase and units. Off to one side was a new dining suite consisting of a glass top table with four chairs.

'Needed to give this flat a good face lift. I even did a bit of smudging.'

'What's that?' Grace suddenly piped up with the question. Carol went over and got her smudging

sticks out. She showed it to both children.

'These are mixed herbs bundled together' she said. You light it and blow out the flame, which leaves the smoke behind. You blow or swirl the rooms in this smoke, especially in the corners which makes everything smell nice and fresh. It also takes away any negative energy and that leaves space for positive energy to enter. Some people may say prayers or chant while smudging. I hope I have achieved gaining positive vibes.'

'You certainly seem to have. The flat smells open and calm and everything is so lovely, new, fresh and gleaming. Not a good time to invite these two over' said Sam, looking at Alfie and Grace while speaking. Alfie looked indigent.

'We are all grown up now, mum!'

'So, you both are,' said Carol. Don't take any notice of your mum.' They both looked at her as pleased as punch.

Carol had bought a cake, snacks and drinks which everyone enjoyed; after which, she took the children to Queenie's flat. 'Come in dears' she said as usual. They spent some time with her, had a look around her flat and then returned to Carol's. Alfie and Grace sat at the dining table playing board games with Queenie while all of them chatted. Carol had also bought them some comics.

'You are spoiling them,' said Sam.

'Who else have I got to spoil? Asked Carol.

'Me!' Said Dave and then blushed.

'I do have something for you'. Carol's tone of voice made Sam look embarrassed.

'That's your mind not mine' giggled Carol. Sam looked even more embarrassed. Luckily, Carol walked away.

They could hear Carol moving around in her bedroom. She returned with a package for each adult. She handed them out.

'Thank you' they all said in unison, as Grace and Alfie also opened their gifts in excitement.

Queenie's was a knitting kit with wool which she had mentioned she liked in passing.

'Lovely! She said. I didn't think you were paying attention to my knitting hobby'. She went over and gave Carol a hug saying thank you again. Dave's was heavy. It turned out to be an encyclopaedia of Handy Tips on DIY, gardening, and more.

'Don't think you need it' said Carol, but I thought you may like it.'

'Thank you. It'll come in handy, I'm sure.'

For Sam, Carol had bought a book on friendship. Sam glanced at it and felt tears stinging her eyes. The words were full of sentiments.

'I mean it', said Carol. I chose it very carefully and especially for you.' They walked towards each other and hugged. They turned around to see everyone looking at them.

'A beautiful book of friendship' mumbled Sam, with a lump in her throat, by way of an explanation.

The James Family did not stay too long, but they all enjoyed their afternoon. Carol asked the children.

'Do you want to leave your games here for another time?'

"Can we come another time?" Asked Alfie in surprise.

'You can come to mine too,' said Queenie. Alfie and Grace were thrilled.

Chapter 30

Carol was happy enough but felt that she needed to do more with her life. She thought about volunteering or something on those lines while walking to the newsagents and small general store, something she hadn't done yet, she'd always driven straight to the supermarket. There she saw a notice in the window saying help wanted. She thought it was a rather old-fashioned request and somehow that drew her to it even more.

'Looking for help?' she asked the older gentleman seated on a high stool behind the counter.

'Yes. But we can't pay you too much.'

'That's ok said Carol. I would like to apply but I don't have any experience.'

An older lady walked in. 'Have you got time to sit and talk?' she asked.

'Yes!' said Carol.

'As you can see, we are really getting too old to be here. Carol didn't know how to reply. Anyway, we are not always busy, but people usually come in for their morning newspaper, especially on a Sunday. It also gets busy when the children come out of the local schools.'

'The older ones can be a hand full' added the older gentleman.

'Which days and times would you need help? Asked Carol.

'Sunday mornings and perhaps a couple of afternoons, just between 3.00 pm and 5.00 pm.'

'I'd love to help', said Carol.

'Really?'

'Yes, said Carol if you'll have me.'

'You haven't asked about wages' said the lady.

'We'll talk about that later. When can I start?'

'Sunday morning 8.00 am'.

'Great! Said Carol. I'll be here.'

The couple slowly dragged themselves to the front of the counter. Bill Robinson shook Carol's hand by way of introduction as did his wife Beryl.

Carol appeared at the shop on Sunday morning. She wrapped her knuckles on the front door and was welcomed in with a smile from Bill. There was a slight rush for newspapers and bread, but it was soon over. Bill offered to make Carol a cup of tea which they were enjoying, as Beryl walked into the shop. The three chatted for a while, just a general conversation.

The more often Carol worked the more at ease she became with the public and quickly learnt about the business from Bill and Beryl. The teenagers who came in and were loud and rude at the beginning began to calm down. Carol figured they were only behaving in that rude manner as it shook Beryl and Bill up and in some perverse way this gave the teenagers a sense of being in control and this brought them enjoyment. Carol was firm with them but not rude. That approach seemed to work. They finally treated Bill and Beryl with respect.

With the first month under her belt Bill said to Carol. 'What are we going to do about paying you some wages, young lady?

'Nothing! I don't want anything. I enjoy working here with both of you' she looked at each of them in turn.

'That's charity! Bill raised his voice. We do not take charity!' Beryl rubbed his shoulder gently.

'Ok said Carol. You can pay me in other ways'.

'How?' questioned Bill. Carol thought fast while looking around this small shop.

'How about I take home a newspaper for a friend and some sweets when I am going to see another friend who has children. Perhaps some bread every now and then'.

Smiling, Bill said. 'That will suit us nicely.' He seemed relieved. Carol was happy that the matter was sorted there and then. Carol took a paper into Queenie after work that day and as always shared her stories of the shop with her.

'That's so kind of you to help them,' said Queenie.

'I wish I could do more' Carol replied. Bill and Beryl slowly became friendlier and Carol in turn felt more at ease as a bonding and trust between them further developed.

Carol was at home one evening when her mobile rung. She assumed it would be Sam or Queenie but it was neither. 'Carol?' asked the voice. She'd just about finished saying hello! so, in that moment she feared for her safety after all that had conspired between her, Ben and Noah.

'We need to talk, said the voice. I am Bill and Beryl's nephew, George.' They arranged a date and time. The place was a coffee shop known to both of them. Carol entered the coffee shop and sensed that the man sitting near the back was George. After quick introductions George asked if she wanted a coffee and went and bought two, then began telling her about the Bill and Beryl.'

'They are my Aunt and Uncle he began. I tried to help them many times over the years but took many knock backs, mostly due to Bill's independence and pride always getting in the way.

'I know something about that', said Carol. George ignored her and carried on.

'Then, last year my wife and I retired so I offered our help again. We could see them getting older and frailer but we were turned down again. In the end I took things into my own hands. It was me that sorted out the newspaper delivery to be brought right to the counter rather than it being left outside the front door and the same being done with other deliveries. They didn't say very much but they appreciated me helping them in that way.

'I did wonder,' said Carol. George carried on.

'I made banking arrangements for their bills to be paid. I started and continue to count and bag their takings and deliver it to the bank myself. They told me about you helping them, so I thought I'd better meet you, especially as you are not getting paid for working at the shop. George suddenly stopped talking as if it was now Carol's turn to speak. He took a sip of coffee and asked, 'more coffee?' Carol guessed it was because his had gone cold. He had been talking for ages.

Carol sat thinking about what to say to him as he went to the shop counter. When he returned, she thanked him for the coffee and asked him what he would like to know about her. He sat across the table from her looking directly into her eyes. She automatically pulled back. George continued staring at her. 'Why are you working in that tiny little shop with two old people? He asked.

'Because I want to' replied Carol.

'You could work in any supermarket and get paid' he said, in no short terms. Carol was finding that this conversation was getting a little annoying now 'Ok! she said. I guess you don't trust me that's fine. I am not however trying to rob, cheat or do anything else to your Aunt and Uncle. I intended doing voluntary work but then I saw their request. I haven't any work training so I felt that this was my opportunity to work and learn at the same time. When I told your uncle, I didn't want payment he told me very clearly that he didn't need charity. I had to think fast so I came up with the idea of taking some items occasionally.'

'I am sure you must know about this, but I keep an account in the till so as Bill's books will tally 'Yes! Yes! George almost spat back. I know all that!'

'Well! What more do you need to know? Carol asked impatiently. George wasn't afraid to ask.

'Why don't you need money?' Carol wasn't about to tell George her life story, so she said calmly

'I am a rich widow!' It was George's turn to pull back in surprise and shock.

'I'm sorry' he mumbled.

'Don't be' snorted Carol. It was a very long time ago. Hence me not having any work experience.

'I see' said George and left the conversation at that.

'Anything else? Carol asked. I take it I can continue working at the shop. If not, I would like Bill and Beryl to tell me that I have to leave.' This was the first time George looked embarrassed.

'I need to protect them' he said, quietly this time.

'I understand said Carol. She stood up. Thank you for the coffee.' She left George at the table watching her walk away.

In time Carol got around to telling Queenie and Sam about her meeting with George. 'I can understand what he was doing, but he could have carried it out in a nicer manner' she said. Her two friends agreed and were pleased to think that Carol's confidence was returning after her rough time with Ben and Noah.

A few weeks later Carol rung Sam with a suggestion, as she put it. 'What suggestion is that?' asked Sam.

'Let's go to a psychic fair. Do you think Alfie and Grace will like it?'

'I have never been to one or ever given it a thought' Sam replied. How about you come over for lunch next week? We'll talk about it then. Are you free Wednesday? Dave is out,' said Sam.

Carol appeared at Sam's on a high. She shoved a newspaper into Sam's hand with it folded showing the advertisement for the psychic fair.

'You read,' said Carol. I'll put the kettle on. Sam noticed that there were a lot of stalls there alongside Mediums giving readings. There were many groups of people from various backgrounds and cultures also due at the venue. 'Looks really interesting, but I don't want the children getting too involved. I think they will like looking at the stalls and it will certainly be a very different way in which to spend the day.'

'Can we go then? Carol was excited, just like a child.'

I'll let you know. Can you leave the paper with me?'

'Of-course' Carol smiled. Tea was ready and Sam fetched some biscuits, lunch was still a while away.

The two women pottered around the garden while they talked and laughed. Carol said that she was still enjoying her little job and that she hadn't seen or heard from George again. 'I don't even know if he told Bill and Beryl about our meeting. There was nothing said by them, so I haven't brought it up.' Soon after lunch Carol left. Sam said that she would let her know about the psychic fair due to take place the following Saturday.

Sam showed the advertisement to Dave. 'Come with us she said. I'll be different, look there are Native Indian Drummers flute players and so much to see and do.'

'You go, take the children' Dave said. You haven't been out anywhere in particular recently. I think Alfie and Grace will like it.'

Sam spoke to Carol and when the day arrived the children couldn't wait to get going.

They watched all the different shaped tents come into view and they could see the glittering and twinkling of items on some stalls. They heard the drums of Native American tribes and couldn't wait to get out of the car and see everything that was unfolding before them. They rushed over to the 'Pow Wow' on display. Carol and Sam watched the children enjoying the display by the Native Indians. They swayed and danced to the music following the lead of the Native dancers, smiling and laughing at each other while taking in the culture and dress. The headdresses of feathers bounced as they stamped their feet to the traditional music in a sea of varied coloured outfits amongst the many tribes. The flute and drumming was new music to their ears as were the tingling bells attached to the dancers' ankles as they danced in their moccasins. They were really pleased to see Alfie and Grace having a good time and doing something different, and as they walked from stall to stall, they looked into the tents. Many new experiences were offered to their eyes, ears and even hearts as each space produced its own good energies.

Grace seemed attracted to a stall selling crystals. She stood and stared at the varied coloured and shaped stones. There were tiny ones, medium sized and others were huge. They all appealed to Grace.

Carol took her hand and asked. 'Do you want to have a closer look?' They both went nearer as Alfie pulled a face. He wasn't interested at all. Sam placed her hand around his neck and led him to Carol.

'I'll walk with Alfie. If we miss each other, we'll meet you there.' She pointed to a gap in between two stalls.

'Hello! Said the lady on the stall. Grace looked up at her. 'You look like an Angel.' Grace lent the side of her body against Carol's and put her arm around Carol's waist.

'Sorry!' Said the lady, I didn't mean to upset your daughter.'

'She's a bit shy' she said and not my daughter.'

'Sorry' said the lady. I really am getting this all wrong.' Carol smiled at her as Grace kept looking at the crystals while still hanging onto Carol. The lady walked over to serve another customer. Carol bent down. 'Are you alright beautiful? Do you want to go somewhere else? Grace took her hand, and led Carol around the stall picking up crystals, looking at them in the light and gently and caringly placing it back on the table, she seemed entranced by them. At last Grace said 'What do you do with crystals, Carol? Or are they just to look at?'

'From what I know said Carol they have different energies within them and they can heal people. My goodness! It suddenly clicked. I am so sorry; you were drawn to them because you are a healer. How could I have not realized that? How stupid of me. Shall we have a proper look? Would you like to have some? Grace's eyes lit up. Would you like big ones or smaller ones you chose?' Grace left Carol's hand and walked around the stall with Carol following her. After looking for a while Carol picked up a small box. Maybe this will help you' she told Grace. She bent down and showed Grace the box holding a collection of small crystals and a book to go with it.

'Can we open it? Carol asked the stall holder.

'Please do' she said. Carol and Grace looked inside; Carol wanted to check. Yes, the book described not only the crystals enclosed but many more. It described their colours, the meanings of the colours and what capabilities and healing power each crystal brings to the human mind, body and soul. 'That's what I want I want to learn,' said Grace.

'Would you like a bigger one as well, or something else? Grace looked at her.

'Don't worry' she said. I'll sort it with your mum and buy Alfie something too.'

'Can we go there? Grace pointed. For her second gift she chose a dream catcher made of feathers to hang at her bedroom window. Later, she told Carol that she also loved all the bangles, bracelets and other jewellery made by the Native American community.

Sam noticed Grace carrying her bag of goodies. Before Grace or Sam could say anything, Carol said. 'Don't say anything Sam its fine. I can take Alfie now and see what he wants. It was too late to stop her, all Sam said was 'See you soon.'

Alfie led Carol back to the stall where they sold Spiritual Cards and Paintings. There were Tarot Cards, Angel Cards and many others. Alfie looked at the Tarot Cards, engrossed, Carol began to get the wobbles knowing that he probably wanted a set, would that meet with his parents' approval, she wondered? She looked around for Sam and Grace. She couldn't see them, but while she was looking, she spotted another stall which she thought Alfie may be interested in. She tried to entice him towards it, but by now he was watching this stall holder putting on a Tarot Card display. He had the cards spread before him and was explaining what the cards in that spread meant. Alfie was captured in the moment. A second spread was laid out and the stall holder explained these to the audience as well. Carol went nearer to Alfie. It was only when the stall holder looked up that she realized, she then did a double take, but there was no doubt, this was George Robinson, Bill and Beryl's nephew who she had decided she didn't like.

'Alright?' she asked Alfie trying to lead him away.

'I'd like those,' said Alfie.

'I don't know if your mum and dad will approve,' said Carol. We'll have to find your mum first.'

'Hello!' George said to Carol. She had no choice but to acknowledge him.

Oh... said Alfie' they will be closing soon'.

'Then let's go back to the other stall, you didn't even look at what it had to offer' she said walking away. Alfie followed, but he was not a happy solider, what he really wanted those Tarot Cards.

'Please Carol he said. I'd really like to learn about the Tarot Cards'. Carol couldn't say no, after all she had just bought Grace exactly what she wanted, and so they went back and bought a set. She paid and thanked George but refused to get into any conversation with him. He now wanted to talk and his attitude and manner had totally changed.

Samantha

The four met up and headed for the car park, where Carol gave Alfie some money, as she had bought Grace two presents.

Alfie and Grace couldn't wait to show their parents what they had bought. They each grabbed their bags and began laying out the items on the dining table as Dave joined them.

Grace placed her crystals and guidebook out alongside her pretty feather dream catcher. Dave

picked up the items and studied them. He glanced at the book, scan reading about the colours, shapes and healing power within each crystal. He admitted to being interested but didn't understand how the elements within the crystals could produce any healing powers.

'I don't understand either dad', said Grace. We can learn together. 'Dave said nothing. He picked up the Dream Catcher and ran his fingers through the feathers.

'Pretty!' he said. Then he seemed embarrassed by his own comment.

Dave looked at the Tarot Cards and the Guidebook. He read about the varied ways in which the cards could be laid out or spread in order for them to be read.'

'I don't like the expression 'reading'. What exactly does that mean? Do you know Alfie?' Alfie looked around confused.

'From what I learned said Sam the image and words on each card explain certain aspects of your life, but it is pretty general and it also depends on which pack of cards you use. There are many to choose from.

'Give me an example,' said Dave.

Poor Carol was worried, she felt as if once again she'd bought trouble into Sam's home. Sam however, decided to play it as a fun idea with the hope that Dave would give his suspicions a rest.

She took the cards, laid out three at random. 'I need the guidebook she said. Those cards have cups on it. She looked at the guidebook. Cups represent love and friendship she read. She looked at the cards again. It means we love each other and we are friends as well.' She winked at Dave.

'I'm sure it's not that simple. You are having me on.'

'Oh! Said Sam. This is a wand and it means many changes. Perhaps there will be, perhaps not. Who knows? I assure you love, once the cards are read each person will interpret the information given to them in the way it suits them best.'

'Not convinced said Dave. Alfie! Grace! He called making sure that they were listening. These gifts are only to be used at home. Don't take them out of the house. Alfie! If Tom is here no Tarot Cards.' They both agreed by simultaneously saying 'Yes dad!'

'I hope you are fine with that Carol,' said Dave.

'Of course,' she laughed nervously.

When alone later, Carol told Sam that she didn't mean to keep bringing strife into her home.

'It's ok said Sam. I suppose we have to accept that Dave will always have his doubts about these things. Let's just hope that neither of the children let us down in the area of their psychic abilities, which I now feel both will continue to pursue as they get older.'

Samantha

Out of the corner of her eye Sam saw Tanya appear. She looked over at her, while reading Tanya's lips with much more ease this time.

'I will be there for both of them' she said. I have yet to make contact with Grace.' Smiling, Sam nodded.

'What's up?' interrupted Dave. You were miles away looking in that corner. I was watching you.'

'That my love is a mystery' said Sam. Carol knew what went on with Sam and Tanya as instinctively the two women walked towards each other and had a hug.

'Women!' Dave mumbled as he left the room for a quiet sit down and a beer.